A Soldier's Dream

1864

Holly Bohling

Bohling, Inc.

Bohling Inc., hollyrbohling@gmail.com

Bohling, Holly R.
    A Soldier's Dream, 1864

ISBN: 978-1-7333788-1-9

Cover Design by Holly R. Bohling
hollyrbohling@gmail.com

Book Design by Holly R. Bohling
hollyrbohling@gmail.com

Dedication

This book is dedicated to our American ancestors who experienced the tragedies of the Civil War from 1861-1865. They were thrust into extreme hardship for many years. Their strength and courage carried us through and helped rebuild a nation that had been torn from within.

Lance Herdegen speaks highly of the American pioneer in his article, "Did the Midwest win the Civil War?" Discussing the evolution of the American pioneer and their changing culture and how it impacted the Civil War, Herdegen states: "In many ways, these settlers and arriving immigrants filling the Upper Middle West were a new kind of American. They had a certain kinship with those who pushed into the Ohio River Valley and Kentucky in earlier times, but they were better educated and riding the growing wave of the Industrial Revolution. They had a sharp sense of place and distance fed by the growth of newspapers, railroads, highways, canals, and the telegraph. They counted among their friends others who were white and black, immigrant or native-born, sons and daughters of local tribes and early French trappers. As soldiers, these "Western boys" had a certain dash and sense of themselves of the like never before seen in the United States. When a Western regiment appeared—one volunteer said— the "fine physique, the self-reliant carriage of its men at once challenged attention." [i]

He ended his article, "It is just as certain now as it was from the very beginning, that America is everchanging and evolving – always a place of new beginnings and fresh starts."

Table of Contents

Prologue

An ancient Sanskrit proverb says: "Yesterday is but today's memory, and tomorrow is but today's dream." Many of you may have heard this before. The next words are just as powerful: "But today well lived makes every yesterday a dream of happiness and every tomorrow a vision of hope. Look well, therefore, to this day."

I've seen many variations of this quote, but the power of his message speaks to each of us personally. Today's experience soon becomes a memory and what we do with these memories directly affects our response in future life experiences. The proverb is just as relevant for us today as it was in ancient times.

Time has three commonly recognized elements, past, present, and future. Putting this ancient quote into the context of our response to life experiences is a thought-provoking exercise. Our response to memories (past) influence how we react in the present and how we build our future dreams.

How quickly time passes, is another element of our experience with time. Some days pass by quickly; others go so very slowly. When re-living a memory over and over, today's experiences become clouded by the cloak of that memory. Once lost in a memory, one can become frozen in time. In this case, the passing of time seems to lose its dimension altogether.

Traumatic experiences have an interesting impact on our daily lives. Often their memories are hard to shake. The violence of war has left a significant scar on generations world-wide. The Civil War had an enormous effect on many American lives. The most widely understood was the abolition of slavery. But there was so much more. It's important to note more men died in the Civil War than any other war in history.

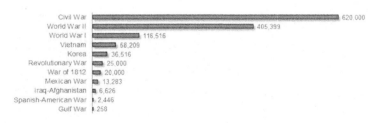

Graph of Military Deaths in American Wars[ii]

Not only did we lose strong young men by the hundreds of thousands, but also many soldiers returned home scarred by war. Many surviving soldiers went west to find gold, homestead, or other opportunities. Many of these men suffered from the horrors of war they'd seen. Shell shock was not recognized for these veterans. It was not understood until World War I. Although Civil War soldiers did not face the horror caused by weapons of mass destruction, they were confronted with the gory violence of hand-to-hand combat. The Civil War was so much more personal. Locally formed, soldiers fought alongside their neighbors, brothers, and cousins, and life-long friends. Too often, they saw their comrade violently killed in battle. Ironically, they may have faced and killed a brother, cousin or friend fighting against them in battle.

Since World War I, historians began to research the experience of the Civil War veteran for symptoms of shell shock, now recognized as post-traumatic stress disorder. Historical records have shown many Civil War veterans faced post-war emotional trauma and were eventually committed to mental asylums filled with war veterans. [iii]

The war within also tore apart the family unit. If not by disagreement in the politics of the war, it was by pulling sons, husbands, and brothers away from home to fight. Friendships ended. Families divided. The war had a direct impact on the farmer's livelihood.[iv] Men too old to go to battle were left behind to work the fields, farming and caring for livestock, counting on their children to help. Many troops that survived the war decided not to return to their home place but went west to find new hope in the future.

Women's lives were changed forever. Southern women were more likely to experience violence and uprisings than those of the north. Many northern women turned to work in the city, finding jobs in munitions factories or jobs that men had held before leaving. Women became doctors and nurses to provide relief to wounded soldiers. Some women even disguised themselves to serve in the war. Others were spies.

Marriage was important to women before the Civil War, even expected. But as the war dragged on, they realized they might never marry as so many men were dying. Many women became spinsters.

Ultimately, women learned to be resourceful and independent. They had to re-evaluate their traditional roles at home, and soon many sought out political involvement and independence. The experience of the Civil War permanently altered women's view of their role in American society.

A Soldier's Dream, 1864

This story is about a young man who grew up in Illinois and joined the Union Army to fight the Civil War. He had already suffered crisis and loss as a young boy growing up in difficult times. Then as a young man, he joined the Union Army as one of the '100 days' men recruited to help President Lincoln bring the war to an end. About 250,000 men from Illinois fought in the Civil War.[v] Records indicate his regiment was assigned to protect the western theater while General Grant secured the eastern theater. The western troops mainly dealt with disease and confederate bushwhackers launching gorilla-type warfare against the union.

Holly Bohling

Chapter 1

Coming Home

<u>**October 1864**</u>
<u>**Ten and Michael**</u>
Slumped in his saddle, Ten groaned as he rested his head on the horse's neck, hoping to stretch his back muscles. It had been a long ride after his regiment was relieved of duty. He stayed with the men until they disbanded in Chicago, where they mustered out. He was headed southwest, and most of the remaining soldiers were headed south. Some men went west to find gold. Ten's eyes closed as he drifted to sleep. He jerked awake as his body began to slip off the horse.

The evening sun was setting as he rode along Little Kickapoo Creek. He was about four hours away from the Fierce home. So close, yet so far. His body shivered with fatigue. His legs continued to shiver as he tried to relax his muscles to no avail. He wanted to be home so badly. To see family, to get a hug, to be warm, and have a hot meal. His mind drifted to the bed he used to sleep on and wondered if it was waiting for him. So much had happened in the last four months. He was different now, and he longed for normalcy.

Ten rode up to a crest of a hill and looked over the valley ahead. Finally, it was familiar country. Daring to look to the future that lay ahead, Ten wondered, "Will anything be the same now?" He anticipated the ride ahead. If he continued into the night, he would see his old bed by late night. Realizing he might startle everyone if he rode up at midnight, Ten pulled up on the horse's reigns and slid off the horse. Sensing they were stopping for the night, the animal seemed relieved as it took a deep breath and let out a long shuddering sigh.

Ten pulled his duffle off the horse, unrolled it, and laid his bedding on the ground. The ground was still covered with fall leaves and would make a soft spot to sleep. He walked over to the creek bed, bringing his horse with him. Ten looked for a deep water pocket near the shoreline and laid down on his stomach. He cupped his hands and splashed water into his mouth. The two travelers took a long slow drink. Finished, Ten stood and led the horse back to the bedroll. Before lying down, Ten rolled in the soft dirt, feigning a dust bath.

Then, sitting in the fading sunlight, and he pulled at the fleas and lice. Removing these pests was a ritual he completed every evening since he began his journey home. Most of the troops at the garrison in Columbia, Kentucky, were covered with these parasites by the time they headed home. He'd gotten rid of the ticks first. This cleansing process reminded him of how hungry, itchy, and hot he'd been. Now that he was on his own, he was able to find rabbits, fish, and berries for nourishment. And, slowly, he was ridding himself of parasites. As the sun sank into darkness, fatigue set in. He sighed deeply, laid down, and instantly fell asleep.

A bright light flashed in Ten's eyes as a young man's pale face loomed before him with blue eyes wide open as his jaw dropped in alarm. Suddenly the man's eyes turned red, with blood dripping down his cheeks like tears. He started laughing and instantly pulled away into darkness. "No!" Ten shouted as he sat up. Startled, his horse took a step back. These dreams came to him every night, usually within the first couple hours of sleep. He so longed for a full night's rest. This man's face haunted him. Ten sat up as he slowly realized where he was. Shaking his head, he slowly lay down and looked through the oak tree branches to gaze at the stars. Ten spoke quietly, "I don't know your name, but it sure seems you're gonna be with me forever. I know you're up there. And I know you didn't do anything wrong." After these dreams, Ten always went over what happened that horrible day, moment by moment. Even though everything happened so quickly, his memory was always in slow motion replay. He couldn't help thinking it through. He tried to figure out what he could have done differently. But he never got that far. His mind blocked him for some reason.

Sitting up, Ten leaned on his knees and listened to the breeze in the trees. The nights were starting to get chilly. He thought about his war buddies. Stationed in Columbus, KY, they were to protect the waterways of the Missouri River while Grant returned to the Eastern Theater with seasoned troops in a campaign to end the war. Because they were part of a rapid recruitment campaign, Ten's regiment was inexperienced and went through a brief training before being deployed. They dealt mostly with small skirmishes against Confederate bushwhackers, small informal bands from Missouri and Kansas hoping to regain Confederate land. Ten figured the bushwhacker he killed was probably his own age.

The captain liked using Ten for his skillful type of informal battle. At 5'2" Ten was short but strong, quick-witted, and fast. Growing up, he'd done a lot of hunting, and like his fellow troopers, he thought it made no sense to stand in a linear formation, totally exposed, shooting at the enemy. At night after a skirmish, the men sat around their campfire and talked about how to fight 'smart.' It made more sense to mimic methods of prey animals in the wild using trees and shrubs as camouflage. Armed with an 1855 Enfield musket, Ten was able to dash, load, and shoot; dash, load, and shoot, repeatedly with speed and agility. He was exceptionally good at it. He was dubbed 'Scramble Ten' by his regiment.

Then that day came, the day Ten would remember the rest of his life. That day, Ten was ahead of the troops, scouting, making his unique dash, load, and shoot pattern while the others advanced behind him.

It was almost too close to shoot. He heard the crunch of leaves, made an abrupt stop and knelt behind a shrub. Crouching behind the shrub, he saw a man's head come up over the western bluff. Ten quietly kneeled to brace himself, hesitated a moment, took aim and fired. The man was nearly 20 feet uphill from him but, to Ten, it seemed like inches. Ten's mistake was to watch the bullet hit his chest on an upward trajectory. Ten saw the blood fly behind the man's head as the pellet exited the back of his neck. The man dropped his rifle and took a few more wobbly steps. Their eyes locked as he came to a stop. He reached for his stomach as blood began to flow out of his mouth. His knees gave out as he sank to the ground, still looking at Ten, but his eyes were no longer in focus. Then he curled over his knees face down on the dirt. Ten had killed plenty of deer and rabbit. But never a human. He remained on his knees, frozen, "Never again... ever!" But he didn't have time to think about it any longer. His regiment was coming up from behind, and he needed to slip through the shrubs in search of other bushwhackers. This man was certainly not alone. As he remembered the moment, Ten continued his thoughts, "If only..." So many things he could have done, so many options he could have taken. "If only..." He was 18 years old and had killed a man.

It usually took Ten a couple of hours to get back to sleep. Over and over, he would think, "If only..." But he always stopped there. In a quiet, steely tone, he asked this haunting face, "You gonna keep comin' back?" There was no answer in the still of the night. "I don't need this." Silence. Alone and on his way home, he realized they would be together for a long time. Ten decided to give this guy a name. In a more friendly tone, he asked, "How 'bout I call you Michael? Tonight, at least tonight, give me a break. No more visits. I just need sleep." He hesitated and said aloud, "If only..." and he dozed off to sleep.

Ten woke with the sound of birds chirping. Sitting up slowly and rubbing his face, he saw his horse watching him. "I guess you're ready to get home. You will like it there." During his time in the regiment, Ten saved his wages, and at discharge, he was able to purchase a horse. Ten named him Smokey. He'd had seen plenty of smoke during the war and thought it would be an appropriate name. "Well, Smokey, got each other, don't we?" The horse followed his new master to the creek and took a drink. Ten scooped a handful of water and splashed his face, then wet his hair, trying to clean up a bit before arriving at Wils' home.

Ten was returning to his brother-in-law's place, Wilson Fierce. That was his home now. Wils had promised him a home, and Ten was forever grateful for Wils' hospitality. They had been neighbors ever since Ten was born back in Ohio. Three families, Fierce, Biggerstaff, and Gibbs, all good friends, moved to Illinois together. They had been so excited about the possibilities in Illinois and moved for the promise of rich farmland. Ten was five years old at the time.

Wils' wife, Lottie, was Ten's oldest sister. When Ten's mother died, Wils' blacksmithing business was booming, and he needed men to help work his farmland. Wils was happy to have Ten, Ten's little brother John, and his pa, Simeon, work the farm, at least until his own boys were old enough to take over. Wils had become like an older brother to Ten, and the men were very close. As Ten left for battle, Wilson saw him off, "Ten, you are a brother to me. You always have a home with us."

Ten stood up from the creek bed and turned to Smokey. With a deep breath, the weary young man hopped on his horse, and the two started back on the trail. They were close and thankfully, this time, the ride would not be long. Approaching the family place, he saw chickens in the yard pecking at whatever treats they could find. The corn harvest was in, and some tidbits were still to be found. Smoke was curling up from the chimney, reminding him of the smell of home-cooked meals. Ten watched another rise of smoke drifting above the smith shop. Ten could hear Wilson's steady clang of his hammer on the anvil. Wils loved creating new equipment for local farmers and found himself much too busy with new orders. He preferred the colder months, as it could get quite hot during the summers with the burning hearth and hot irons.

A Warm Hello
The family was busy and didn't see Ten riding up to the house. He swung his leg over the saddle and

unloaded his gear from the horse's back. As he set it on the ground, he heard his name, "Ten!" Lottie cried out as she stepped out to investigate the sounds at her front door. "You're home!" She ran to him and hugged him.

He grabbed her, and they swung around. "Lottie, it's so good to see you!" Ten's big sister had become a mother to him over the years. She was 11 years old when Ten was born, and when their mother died, she was 24 years old and married, Ten was 13. Now, seven years later, she was 31 and already had five children. Ten looked closely at his sister. In the four months he was gone, she had changed. She looked so weary. "Did she look this tired when I left?" Ten wondered.

She noticed that he was concerned and stepped back to change the subject before he could say anything. She looked at him, "Ten, you look terrible! It's like hugging a bag of bones! Come in and let me feed you. Duke, go get Wils." Duke groaned in protest as he turned and ran over to the smith shop. Lottie had named her oldest son Wellington. Charlotte loved the elegant name, but Wils did not respond well to the idea. "But Wils, we can call him Duke, as in the Duke of Wellington." She argued, "The Duke was such a grand hero! Our firstborn son deserves a grand name!" Wils conceded if he could call him Duke.

As the two headed inside the house, the children stopped running about to stare at the stranger. The older ones remembered Ten and paused for a moment, and then dropped their mouth in surprise when they realized who he was. Ten's hair and beard had grown long; he was dirty and thin. His clothes hung limply over his shoulders. But they didn't care; they dashed forward to hug him ignoring the dirt and mess. Ten was thankful he'd spent every night of his journey cleaning up what he could. "Ten, you're home!" Children shouted, jumping and dancing around him. The little ones joined in the fun. Ten could only laugh as he tried to hug each of them, one at a time, and they ended up in a group hug.

Lottie smiled, "They'll keep you busy." She took his arm to escort him into the house. "Come in and sit!"

"Sounds good!" He smiled, "Let me take care of Smokey first."

"No," Lottie said, "Let Duke take care of that; you've been on the road a long time."

He turned back to look at Smokey, "I'd like to do it. It won't take long." Ten took Smokey's reins and guided his horse through the new yard that would be his home. "You'll like it here, Smokey."

He took his horse to the barn, removed the saddle and blanket, and filled the feed bucket. He spent a good hour brushing his horse down. As they traveled home, Smokey had heard Ten yell out every night. Then he would watch and wait for Ten to fall back to sleep. The two had a bond. Ten felt this animal understood his hauntings more than any human ever would, and he vowed to take care of his comrade for all the horse's life. The warmth of the horse felt good to Ten's hands as he continued to brush it down in the cool barn. Ten lost track of time. It had been a while since Smokey had some quality care, and both relished the moment together. In a few minutes, Duke came out, "Ma said it's ready. Need help?"

Ten looked up, realizing he'd taken too long. "I'm done. Let's head on in. Looking back to Smokey, "You rest now." Ten said as he slapped the horse on his rump. It was hard to walk away from his horse; they'd been together for so long. He turned back to Duke, and the two walked side by side toward the house. Ten asked, "You've grown in the short time I was gone! How old are you now?"

Duke responded, "Thirteen, Ten. I'm the same age as when you left!"

Ten laughed, "Ah, ha-ha. I feel I've aged five years and figured you did too!"

The children bustled around Ten as he stepped in the house. He barely had a chance to settle the children and sit at the dinner table when Wils burst into the room. "Ten!" he shouted. Still worn out from the ride home, Ten slowly pushed himself up out of the chair to greet his brother-in-law. The two stood side to side, slapping each other's backs with one hand while shaking hands with the other. They kept smiling and laughing at... nothing. "Tell me, Ten. How was it?" Wils asked as he sat down on the chair next to Ten's. Ten's countenance slowly changed from joy to fatigue.

"It wasn't good." Ten replied, "No one should ever go through that. The killing.... it makes no sense." He sat down while Lottie began to move about the kitchen. She pulled some eggs out of the fresh egg basket to throw in the spider pan. The three-legged iron pan was heavy, and she used both hands on the long handle as she carried it to the table. Carefully, she set it down next to the eggs. Concerned, Ten watched her and went on, "Guess I'd rather not talk about it right now. Maybe one day." Changing the subject, he asked, "What's been happening here!"

Wils continued, "I understand Ten. This war has gone on too long. We've lost too many of our young men. I'm glad you came home. I hear it's about over now and I hope that's true. These days, we just can't predict what will happen next."

"Aw, I didn't see too much battle." Ten replied. "Compared to others, that is. But I saw enough. How's smithin'?"

"It's going very well. I am blessed and looking for a good partner to help."

"I'd be glad to do it!" Duke brightened up.

"No Duke, first thing you need to learn is farmin'." Wils turned to Ten, "Your food comes from farmin'. Smithin' can come later. It's not just shoeing horses. That only takes up about a fourth of my time. I spend more time coming up with ideas, designing what new machinery these farmers want before I can do any smithin'. I've been doing a lot of horse-drawn hay rakes and reapers. There's folks with money asking for these things. They are buying land and can afford to pay for this equipment. It's good for me." He paused. "But it's hurting small farmers. They can't compete; prices are dropping. Bigger farmers produce so much more, and grain companies are charging farmers to store it til the trains come through. On top of all that, I hear property taxes are still going up! So many of the small farmers can't make it so they are moving west to homestead. But nobody's talking about that. Right now, all they talk about is the war. When the war is over, the talk will shift to the movement west."

Ten added, "A lot of the guys in my regiment are headed west, to homestead or find gold."

Lottie had finished putting little Nellie and Jessie down for bed and came down the loft ladder. She stumbled on the last step and caught herself quickly. Ten watched her recover as she walked back to the table. "Okay everyone, it's late and time for bed. The sun is down, and it's dark out there. Duke, you take the older children out to the bathroom and make sure there is no fighting." Duke groaned as he stood up. "Take the shotgun with you; I saw coyote scat this morning."

Sarah let out a screech when she heard that. "I don't want to go out."

Lottie sighed, "Okay, you can use bed-pans, but, Sarah, you will have to empty them in the morning."

"Eew!" Sarah complained, but she knew it was a better plan than going out in the dark.

"I get the window tonight!" Margaret hollered as she ran out the door in front of Duke. She had the most spunk and was always ready to take on coyotes, and of course, her older sister and brother.

The children shared one large mattress filled with corn husks. They slept on the same mattress, alternating head to toe. Half slept with their heads by the window, and the other half slept with their heads towards the loft railing. Lottie had made a quilt filled with a thin layer of feathers to cover the mattress. Their bed was on one end of the loft. Wils and Lottie were on the other end with a curtain draped between them and the children. As Duke got older, none of the children wanted to sleep next to him as he was always stretching out, flopping over and bumping them. Wils and Lottie had decided when Ten came back, Duke could sleep over in the bunkhouse if he wanted. But for now, Duke took the end closest to the center ladder. This also made it easier for him to slip down the ladder and get an early start on morning chores.

All of Duke's siblings wanted the window and would often complain about sleeping between people and waking up with a toe in their face. At least they had less chance of that when they had the window on one side. Lottie made sure they took turns.

As the children worked their way out the door to the outhouse, Wils looked at Ten, "I'm sure glad you came back. I need you in the fields. Our fall harvest didn't turn out so good. You know what to do out there, and Duke is ready to learn details to make it work. My boys need to learn it right."

Ten was glad to hear this. He wanted to keep busy. He needed to prevent Michael from surprising him during waking hours. Occasionally during lonely quiet moments, Michael would rise up even when Ten was awake. That was one reason why he didn't want to talk about the war. With just the thought, he could feel Michael simmering, waiting to show his face again. He looked at Wils, "Well, I'm ready."

"Now Ten," Lottie interrupted as she cleaned the dinner mess, "You need to rest a few days and fatten up. Then we will let you get out there."

"No, Lottie, you don't understand. I need to stay busy." His quick response was more than intense. Lottie watched him closely, trying to figure out what Ten meant by that. She went on picking up the used dishes from the table.

"I can fix you a fine breakfast tomorrow. But don't expect it every day. Our chickens have been laying pretty good this year since we started keeping them in the barn at night. I won't have any gravy for you, but I can have the next day."

Ten brought up Pa, "I do want to go up and see Pa. How's he doing?"

"Not good, Ten." Lottie answered. "He should never have enlisted. He's too old. They knew he wasn't 47 years old, and they still let him in." She was angry but knew there was nothing she could do.

"Lottie," Wils interrupted, "He was desperate. He's lost everything; this was one way he could get some money."

"Well, I don't know why he went off and married this Jane woman, either." Lottie continued. "He's not making good decisions!"

Ten wondered about Jane too. He listened and knew this must have been a conversation Wils and Lottie had nearly every night since his Pa married Jane so soon after Ma died. He also knew Pa was desperate in very tough times. "I understand Lottie; but I see why he enlisted. Yes, I know he knew Lincoln personally, and wanted to fight for our country and support the President. And yes, it brings a good pension. But, I think, most of all, he needed to show he was still a man."

Ten tried to settle the argument about Jane, either. "I don't like that he married Jane. She can't bring in enough money doing laundry and baking to take care of all her own kids, let alone Pa and little John. I wonder if mustering in helped him get away from Jane."

After a long pause, "Hadn't thought of that." Lottie quietly replied.

Wilson looked down, paused a moment, and then looked back at Ten. "Ten, your pa's leg is festering with infection. It seems he fights it off, and then it gets worse. Jane sounds like she is angry she has this added burden caring for him on top of the kids. Last time I rode up there, she was trying to find a place to send him. She says she can't afford him, even with his pension."

Ten was alarmed. He hadn't counted on Jane's rejection. He knew Pa and Jane needed each other but had thought or hoped; there was some sort of affection between them. "Evidently not." Ten thought to himself. He spoke out loud, "I need to get up there pretty soon, then. I will help clear the timber and get some ready for burning this winter. I saw some overgrowth on my way in... and I can do a few repairs before cold sets in. Then I want to head on down there before spring planting season, see how pa is doing, and find out what I can do to help."

It was early yet, but Ten wanted to stoke a fire in the bunkhouse, warm up the building and arrange his things. Lottie knew he would be coming, so she already had the bunkhouse clean and ready for him. The bed was made up. He was glad he didn't have to share it with anyone, for now. He was tired of sleeping so close to the other men in the regiment all the time. Listening to them snort and snore all night made it impossible to sleep. And these days, he didn't know how much noise he made when Michael visited. He preferred to keep that to himself.

About two in the morning that night, Wils woke up to a loud yelp. "What in God's name was that?" he thought. He sat awhile listening to the silence. Not a breeze was stirring as the night cold had settled over the house. Lottie rolled over in her sleep. Wils got up and walked around to see if anything was amiss. He peeked in at the children, who were all asleep, then walked down the ladder and around the first-floor rooms. He dreaded stepping outside as it was cold. It would take him a long time to warm up again. He added some timber to the stove, welcomed the heat as he tossed the logs on the fire, then stepped out the front door for a quick look. Opening the door, he saw the moon shone bright over the yard. In the bunkhouse, he saw a lamp light up. It was then he realized the yelp he heard was from Ten. "Interesting," Wils thought. "I wonder what caused that? We may want to wait a while before letting Duke sleep over there. Let's see what happens."

The next day, Ten was out early in the morning, already nailing loose boards inside the barn when Wils came out to see him. Winter was setting in, and it was good the hens would have some protection from the cold. He opened the barn door. "Hey Ten, come on in for some coffee. We're up."

"Thanks, Wils, I just thought I'd get this little piece fixed before coming in. I fed the chickens already."

Wils smiled as he stepped back into the house and turned to Lottie as she prepared breakfast. "It's good to have him back."

Wils woke their oldest son, Duke. "Time to come on down." The four ate breakfast quickly and quietly. They wanted to get back out to work before the younger children woke up. The peace and quiet of the morning would not last once they came down.

As they finished, Ten stood, "If you don't have anything else, I want to start on that wheat and clear that overgrowth in the timber. I'll ride along the fencing to look for repairs along the way."

"Ten, just take at least a day to rest up; you need to gain some weight!" Lottie protested.

"I'm just fine, Lottie. I need to keep busy." Ten said. He stood up, nodded politely, took a few steps back, and turned to leave.

After Ten closed the door behind him, Wilson turned to Lottie. "Lottie," Wilson said quietly, "Did you hear him last night?"

"No, what do you mean?"

"He let out a horrible scream in the middle of the night. I didn't know what it was, so I got up to see what was going on. As I stepped out the door, I saw him light the lantern in the bunkhouse. I knew it was him."

"I wonder what that's about?" Lottie asked.

Wilson responded. "Something must have happened. He has a lot to work through. If I were him, I'd be out there clearing that overgrowth too. It'll do him good."

"Well, we'd better wait before letting Duke sleep over there." Lottie thought out loud, then she added, "Let Ten work it out first." Wils nodded.

Ten found the ax in the barn, threw it into the wagon, and hitched his horse. He pulled his jacket close to keep warm and climbed up on the wagon. "It'll be good to get this over before winter. They need a good supply of firewood anyway. Maybe I can get enough to take down to Pa." He pulled the wagon up to the edge of the timber and stepped into the overgrowth. A deer leaped out of the shrubs, startled by Ten's approach. Ten jumped higher than the deer. "I'm so jumpy," he thought as he tried to settle his heart.

He decided to start from the outside and work his way into the timber. He was surprised how much had overgrown in the short time he was gone. "Or maybe," he thought, "I just didn't see it." He found a dead pine tree and decided to start with that. Studying the tree and the land, he planned for the direction of the tree's fall. As he swung at the trunk, he felt the release of tension built up during his journey home. Each hit seemed to release a wave of negative energy. By the time Ten cut the wedge into the trunk, he found it easier to forget Michael's visit the night before. At least for a moment.

Moving to the other side of the tree, he began to chop at the trunk, aiming to shape a wedge a third of the way into the tree. "Whack." Each swing felt good. The ax handle pulled on his callouses as it hit the trunk, threatening to build blisters underneath the callouses. Ten didn't care. It just took a few minutes for the tree to begin to sway and groan. Ten stepped back to look up, decided all was well and took another whack at the trunk. The tree groaned some more and slowly began to tip. Bit by bit, the weight of the tree began to pull over. It picked up speed as it fell, landing with a loud thud. The ground vibrated across the timber. Ten's horse shuddered but stood in place. Ten smiled with satisfaction, walked over to his horse, and said, "Good boy, you can stick around!" Ten sat down on the wagon to rest a moment. He pulled out some bread and jerky Lottie had given him. He found hunger came quickly, and the food felt good. Taking a swig of water from his canteen, he grabbed the cut saw from behind his spring seat to saw the tree into logs for the horses to pull back to the house. Bucking and splitting the logs into firewood would come later back at the house.

He took a day off clearing timber to train Duke to harvest potatoes and prepare them for winter storage. "Ok, Duke, be careful; these tubers are fragile. See how easily the skin breaks? Use a pitchfork to dig from the side of the plant. Once you're deep enough, lift the soil from underneath the plant. Then work from the bottom to loosen the potatoes and gently set them aside. Remember, this will be your dinner next year, and you don't want them to spoil!"

The two weeks that followed were a blessing for Ten. He loved the predictable routine of getting up and heading back out to clear the timber. No sudden orders from the Captain changing their plans on a moment's notice. No one was telling him what to do. Peace and quiet. The tedium was good. Each morning he could direct his thoughts before getting up to plan chores of the day. He was getting much better at managing Michael. As days were more predictable, peaceful, and physically active, the less intense were Michael's visits. Today, he was cutting tree trunks into firewood. After cutting up two trees, he had a good pile of firewood out front of the Fierce home. The next project would be splitting logs. Clouds started building in the sky on the sixth day. Seeing the storm clouds pile high made Ten nervous. The lightning and thunder triggered memories of gunshots and cannons. So, he prepared a chore list for the next day to keep his mind busy. As he sat down at the dinner table, Ten said, "Wils, looks like a storm is coming. I won't be splitting logs tomorrow. What do you say, tomorrow, I butcher one of those hogs for winter?"

Wils took a bite of egg and chewed as he looked at Ten. "Ten, take a break. It's Sunday. Let's go to church tomorrow. Have you been since you left?"

"Not much opportunity."

"Okay, tomorrow, after breakfast, we'll be off to church, and you must join us. Folks will be glad to see you. Monday, you can butcher the hog."

Ten was uncomfortable sitting in the church hall as he kept an eye on the storm clouds in the distance. The last time he sat in church, he was with Wils, Lottie, and the kids. He was young and had not yet felt the scars of war. And now, he'd killed a man. He squirmed in his seat as he suppressed the memory of a red-eyed boy. "Michael will surely visit me tonight," he thought. Even the reverend's message of forgiveness didn't appease him. The peace he sought turned into guilt for the deeds of war.

The Fierce family usually stayed at church all day eating and spending time with friends. Ten rode Smokey to church, and found an excuse to slip out early, advising the others to head home soon before the storm hit. Wils watched him ride away. "He will get used to us again," Wils thought.

Sure enough, as Ten fell into a slumber that night, the thunderstorm sounded its's fury as Michael's face flashed before him with the same vivid eye sequence. Five times those eyes haunted him that night. Five times Ten awoke to his own screams. It was too much for Ten. Exhausted, he refused to go back to sleep. He dressed and slipped outside into the predawn darkness, checking on Smokey.

The days passed. One day Ten would be out splitting logs, another day, he'd be mending the barn roof. He'd butchered one hog, and Lottie processed the meat for the winter. The cellar was nearly filled. They would have a solid winter. If a blizzard shut them up for a few days, all would be fine. Wils joined Ten as they headed into the house one evening. Loaded with orders for his blacksmith shop Wils gave Duke the okay to learn some ironwork as well. Ten had no interest in it. "Too hot for me!" Ten said. "I'd rather be out in the fields, smelling the air and watching the corn break through the soil. I love the race against time to produce that corn by fall."

Thankfully Wils put a hand on Ten's back as they walked into the kitchen. "I am so glad we got you back in time to get us ready for winter. It gave me a chance to get these orders done. Smithin' is busy these days. We will have a good year because of you!" Ten smiled. Wils stopped walking causing Ten to look back at him, "Ten, I know I've said this before, but I mean it. You are family. You, Phietta, John, I love you all. You can stay here as long as you want."

"Thanks, Wils, I 'preciate that." Ten looked down as they stepped into the house. These moments were awkward for him. Wils was a good man and took care of Simeon's kids the best he could. Ten thought of his sister, who was living in a town nearby, "How is Phietta, anyway. Have you heard from her?"

Wils paused, "Yes, a lot has happened over there. Sam left her. He wanted more in life and went west for gold. I heard he was in Idaho somewhere. We send her money occasionally; and told her she could live with us. She said he promised to send money. Right now, she is waiting to hear from him"

Ten's eyes opened wide to hear Phietta's news, but he was not surprised to hear Lottie and Wils were helping her. The two sisters were close. "I haven't even been gone a year!" he exclaimed. "You know

Wils, when we were discharged, I heard a lot about men going west without their family. You know, many don't send for their loved ones to join 'em. I don't know what happens to them. Do they die? Find another woman? Who knows?" Ten hesitated, "Let me know how I can help. I can help bring her things here. "

Wils smiled, "You and I think a lot alike. I'd like to get an extra building up for her and the kids. We have space," he paused, "and between you, me, and Duke, we could get something up pretty quick."

Ten responded as he stood up, "I'll watch for some good logs as I clear the timber."

Wils wanted to tell him more, "Things were a bit stormy over there. Sam was not interested in farming. She was happy. He kept talking about going west to find gold. I think he felt tied down by the children." Ten remembered Sam but didn't know him very well. Sam was older, like Wils, Charlotte, and Phietta. It wasn't the same as Wils, who made a point to know Ten. Ten was a young boy, and Sam was just another grown-up. However, he did feel close to both Phietta and Lottie. When their ma died, only two children were left with Simeon, Ten and John. The rest had already left home, like Lottie, Phietta. They were already married when their mother became ill. Both Phietta and Lottie stepped in to help Ten and his little brother, John. Simeon, Ten, and John moved in with Lottie and Wils, who became like parents to the boys. Phietta helped Lottie as much as she could taking, Ten and John for summer vacation and extended visits.

Wils interrupted Ten's thoughts. "Ten, let's make a deal. I have the land but can't work it. Thanks to you, we will have plenty of food on the table, plus income from the harvest." Ten was more than a farm laborer. He was smart, strong, and could manage the farm. Most of all, he was family, Lottie's brother. "I've always admired how took over your Pa's farm while your Ma was dying... and you were only 13. Now that you're working the fields and livestock full time for us, let's make a business deal." The two agreed, Ten would get 50% of all farm crop profits. It was generous, but Wils pointed out this would give Ten a chance to build up a savings to break out on his own.

"Thanks, Wils, I would like to save up for my own place." Ten answered dryly. Frankly, Ten hadn't thought much about it, but he knew it was the answer Wils wanted to hear.

The New Year holiday was bitter cold, and Ten became restless with little to work on during the bitter stormy days. He could only mend tools and leather goods so many times. The children took care of the chickens and small chores around the yard.

News of the war came along on Sundays before and after church. Ten began staying on a bit longer to chat with the other farmers and get the local gossip. Still, he could only take so much. He had his own war battling in his head and did not want to hear the continuous opinions regarding Lincoln and General Grant's decisions. Once he listened to the newest updates, he lost interest as people would get heated in their opinions. His eyes would glaze over, and he would step away to wander off by himself.

It was a drizzly day the first of February 1865, when Ten decided to take 160 pounds of potatoes from the cellar to sell in town. He was hoping to get some cash to take with him when he went up later to visit Pa. He arrived outside the general store and found the hustle a bit overwhelming. He kept his eyes down as he slipped off the wagon, swung the reins over the post, and went to the back of the wagon to untie the tarp. A door at the saloon down the street slammed shut, causing Ten to jump and spin toward the noise. In a flash, he saw Michael's blood-red eyes. He swayed as the sight of Michael's eyes disoriented him. In the next moment, the vision disappeared. Ten knew the noise was nothing, but his body reacted anyway. He hated Michael's interruptions during waking hours. Ten glanced around pretending to show interest in the activity of town and was relieved. It appeared folks hadn't noticed as they kept on with their business. Still, he was embarrassed. Flushed, he turned back to untying the tarp, took a deep breath, and grabbed a handful of potatoes. Forcing a smile, he stepped into the general store to greet the shop owner. "Hi Les."

"Well, look at you, Ten Gibbs!" Les stepped from behind the counter, "I heard you were back. It's so good to see you!" Les repeated himself, "It's sooooo good to see you!" and he grabbed Ten's hand and shook it vigorously. Ten smiled miserably, waiting for the shaking to end.

"Hi Les," he replied, trying to be cheerful. "I've brought about 160 pounds of potatoes for you."

"That's great, Ten. Actually, Doc Hanson's wife was just here. With their eight kids, they pretty near wiped me out. Bring 'em in."

Ten returned home with four dollars in his pocket, $2.00 for Wils. That left $2.00 for him. He was thrilled.

February 1865 was a bitterly cold month. Early that month, a cold night wind blew. Dark clouds were forming overhead, and an intense storm appeared to be setting in. Ten went out to bring in more firewood for the house then took a load over to the bunkhouse. Lottie told the children to set out the bed pans, so no one had to go to the outhouse. The children had the chore of emptying used pans when the storm was over. He tied a rope from the outhouse to the bunkhouse, from the outhouse to the house, and finally from the house to the barn. This would help them navigate without getting lost. The bunkhouse was connected to the barn so Ten didn't need a separate rope to the house. The rope would guide them navigate during the storm without getting lost. He secured the livestock and headed back in for dinner. Now, one must wait for the storm to pass.

Lottie gave Ten enough food to last a couple of days. "Depending on the storm, I may come on over for company in the morning. If you skim the cream, I'd be glad to do some churning for you." Ten said as he stepped out the door with his arms loaded with food. Lottie was thrilled for the help. Churning was a tough job.

Fine thin and frigid snow burst in as he opened the door. He grabbed the rope and lifted it slightly to wrap his left arm around it, while juggling his food in the other. "Looks like a blizzard." Ten paused as he tucked his head down and walked out into the storm.

Wils and Lottie stepped back in out of the cold blast. "See you tomorrow." Lottie smiled, "It will be nice to have your company." Ten shivered and continued his trek in the blinding white snow.

Alone in the bunkhouse, Ten needed to keep busy. He brought in his saddle, tack, and gear to clean and oil during the storm. He also brought in twine to make ropes. "I will head out to see Pa as soon as things clear up. It's taking me too long. If the weather would let up..." He went on to think through his chores, creating a timeline of what to accomplish before heading out to see Pa.

At dinner that next night Ten went over to eat with the others. Although it was below zero and the wind was still causing snowdrifts, it had stopped falling. At dinner, he brought up his plan to visit Pa. Simeon's place in Persifer was about 30 miles due north of them. "As soon as the weather clears, I'd like to go see Pa. Would it be alright if I take them some firewood and dried ham?" Ten asked.

"Absolutely Ten," Lottie said right away. She also worried about her pa. She wasn't so sure his second marriage had been a good idea. He couldn't take care of the combined families. Lottie had wanted him to stay with them. "I have a quilt for them too. I'd love it if you take it up to him. I worry he is getting chilled with the cold winds."

"I was thinking of getting down and back before planting season. It's a short window." Ten added, "I might stay a few days to help them a bit. I know I don't belong there with Jane and her kids. But I suspect Pa could use a little help."

Lottie responded, "Sounds good. I'll write and tell them you are coming."

Ten took the next couple of days to load the wagon, cover it with a tarp and tie it down. Last, he greased the wheels for easier pulling. By the first of March he was ready and hitched Smokey to the wagon. "Thanks so much," Ten nodded to Lottie and Wils as he settled onto the wagon. "I will be back soon."

Chapter 2

Memories

It took one night and two days to get to Persifer. It was only a 30-mile ride due south from Cambridge, but they were pulling a wagon, and he wanted to take it easy on Smokey. Smokey walked at a steady rhythm lulling Ten into his thoughts. Memories flooded his mind. He watched his mother die during harvest. Going to the fields alone as his father cared for her. In the end, he moved in with Wils and Lottie. Pa married Jane so quickly after Ma died. And then, of all things, Pa joined the Union Army when he was too old to go. It just didn't seem right. And now, his siblings were off and gone. It was a challenge to stay in touch with them anymore. They wrote Wils and Lottie letters, and he read those. For Ten, it seemed like things just didn't matter anymore. He thought it was better to stay safe and not love anyone. Ten spoke aloud "Smokey, why bother? They all die eventually." His horse whickered in response to Ten's voice and kept on walking without missing a beat.

Michael, the night visitor, simmered in his thoughts as he rode. The visitor tried to pop up with his gory image. But Ten suppressed it. While awake, he was getting quite good at sensing Michael's efforts to show his face, and Ten had developed tricks to push back the visitor. If he felt Michael pushing out, Ten would analyze his next job, break it into steps, complete with a supply list and timelines. His visitor only broke through when Ten's guard was down or when he was asleep. Ten found this ride was more difficult than he expected. He went on talking to Smokey, 'I wonder if Wils and Lottie have heard me at night. I know I'm noisy, it even wakes me up." Smokey kept his pace.

The night was going to be very cold. As the sun went down, he came to a stop under some trees and built a fire for warmth. He had brought a cowhide for warmth and wrapped himself in it while he ate some jerky and beans. "Next time, I need to take this trip in the summer." Ten told himself. "Even in the army, weather was better than this." Thoughts about the army immediately triggered the familiar memory of his visitor. He shook the image out of his head, wrapped himself tightly and went to sleep.

Sure enough, those bloody eyes greeted him that night. He awoke with a cry, so forlorn Smokey whinnied, shook his head, and pawed the ground. "Sorry, Smokey." Ten said quietly, as he lay back down.

Ten arrived mid-afternoon that second day. He pulled up to a small house on the edge of town and jumped down from the wagon. He tied his horse to the post out front and walked up to the door. He hesitated to take a deep breath before knocking. It wasn't long before Jane opened the door. "Oh, it's you." She turned and walked back into the house. "Ten's here." She hollered as she walked away. Ten stood in the doorway a moment, not sure what to do. "Close the door, it's chilly out there." Jane hollered back. Ten obediently stepped in and closed the door. "You'll have to put up your horse down at the stable at the other end of the street. Might do that first so you can get him settled in."

"I'd like to say hi to Pa first." Ten said as he took another step.

"Ten, is that you?" Ten heard his pa speak weakly from the back room. "Come on back. I want to see you!"

Pa was lying in bed in obvious pain. He was too thin and white as a ghost. "It's no better, huh?" Ten asked.

Pa looked down at his left leg. He'd been shot in his upper thigh, and the injury was just not healing. "Yea, it just keeps flaring up; makes me sick. I can't keep any food down. Chicken broth works best. That bullet did a number in there."

Ten winced to see his pa suffering. "I brought some firewood and Lottie sent dried ham. Looks like Jane and the kids can eat the ham. Sorry, I didn't bring any chicken."

"You'd better get your horse shut in for the night." Jane reminded him from the front room.

Ten stood up, "I'll be right back Pa," as he backed out of the room. He stepped out the front door without a word, unloaded the wagon, and carried supplies inside. Jane looked at him, took the ham, and said thanks. Again, she turned her back on him. "You can stay for dinner and the night, but we don't have room to keep you any longer." Ten nodded and went back out to take his horse to the stable. It was still light, but the sun's rays began turning to gold as he returned to the house. He had dried ham and a biscuit as he spent the evening in his pa's room. Ten helped him sit up to give him some broth. Simeon dozed off quickly. Ten sat watching him a while longer until he heard that the children were all put to bed. He stepped out to the kitchen and said to Jane. "I'll leave first thing in the morning."

"I know you think I'm terrible," Jane answered as she cleared the dinner table. "I just can't take care of him on top of the kids. I'm trying, but I just can't do it. I take in laundry and bake, but it's not enough." She was near tears. "I hadn't planned on this when we married." She tipped her head towards Simeon's room. "His pension helps, but it's not enough. I've got kids and now I'm his nurse." She waited for Ten to respond. Ten slowly sat down in a wooden chair. She went on, "There's a place for veterans up in Rockford, a home for wounded soldiers. I wrote them, and they said they can take him. I'm going to send him up there."

Ten straightened up. "Jane, I'll take him." He was thrilled with the idea. His pa would be out of here and in a place where he would be well fed, and they will take good care of him. Maybe he would even get better! "I need to get back to Wils and for plantin'. But I'll be back in early August when it's not so cold and I've got a break. I'll rig a little canopy over the wagon."

Jane stopped and thought a moment. There was silence while she considered the idea. Ten sat waiting for her to consider her options. "Okay, I can wait til then. You come back early August. I will write and tell them you will be bringing him then."

Ten brought his bedroll into the house and laid on the floor by the stove. "Actually," Ten thought, "This was better than what he had during the war."

Long about two in the morning, that familiar face popped into his dreams. Ten lurched up with a yell. Disoriented, he looked around the room, trying to recall where he was. He heard a thump from Jane upstairs as she hollered, "What was that?"

He moaned silently to himself, then replied, "Nothing, just had a bad dream." Jane responded with silence. Thankfully the children slept through the commotion.

Ten tossed and turned the rest of the night. Worrying about his pa, wanting to help Wils, there were too many things to do in so short a time. With the first chirp of the morning birds, Ten quietly sat up and rolled his bedding. He peeked in at his pa, who moaned in his sleep. Ten shook his head as he turned to leave. He added timber to the stove to heat the house when they got up and quietly slipped out the door. Ten walked down to get Smokey and left some coins for payment. Smokey was glad to get out of the stables. The stables reminded Smokey of the days before Ten, when by strange unpleasant humans surrounded him. He was happiest on the road with Ten, just the two of them. He knew they were heading back out. Ten took Smokey back to Jane's, hitched the wagon, and rolled out of town before the sun's rays began to peek from the eastern horizon.

They took the same route home, stopping in the same spots. The return trip seemed faster as Ten began preparing a list in his head of what needed to get done before coming back for his pa.

Back home with Wils, Ten was excited to prepare the land for planting. Each morning began with chores while Lottie fixed breakfast. After chores, he looked forward to breakfast. On pleasant days they ate outside at a large table. When the weather was bad, they ate inside. They would eat and head right back out to work the fields and care for the livestock. Lottie would send the girls out with a mid-morning lunch to where Ten and Duke were working. Noon dinner was their big meal. Lottie would clean up and, frequently, she would churn while the rest were outside. Evening was usually a light supper as the sun went down. Everyone was tired and the family took some time to discuss the day's work, upcoming plans and priorities.

The winter blizzards and snowdrifts had been rough on the fence rails. Some needed replacement, others just secured. Ten started with the hog pen while the chickens ran wild and got underfoot. Ten tried to shoo them off with his leg as he lifted new rails onto the supports. On rainy days he focused on equipment repairs in the barn. Ten's goal was to get the potatoes in as soon as he could. He was thankful for Duke's help, Lottie's oldest son. He could move faster with help from Duke. It was little Francis's job to keep the chickens away and run errands. Duke was not the most motivated helper. He wanted to be a blacksmith and spent as much time as he could with Wils in the shop. Wils wanted Duke to learn farming which caused some tense family discussions. "Ten is about the best young farmer I know, Duke. I want you to learn as much as you can from him while he is with us."

"But Pa, I love making machinery like you. You're always talking to people; they even come out to see you. You're important."

Wils reached out his hands and shoved up his sleeves, "Duke, look at the burns on my hands. It's a hot, sweaty job, especially in the summer. Every day it's the same thing, stoke the fire and beat the iron, day after day. I can't see storms blowing in.

Farming changes with every season and with every storm. Your days are always changing."

Ten thought, "That's interesting; I thought farming was tedious. I like that to watch the weather, I can sense what's coming and plan for it. But maybe Wils is right, a farmer must, on a moment's notice, catch the cow, kill the snake, or race against the hailstorm to bring in the harvest. I guess that is the adventure!"

He looked at Duke, "Hey Duke, let's go out and get the fences done before dark sets in completely. Then I'll show you how to trim the Apple trees in the morning." He stood up and put a hand on Duke's shoulder. The two headed out. "I'd also like to work with you and the girls on the garden. If you plant things right, they bear much better fruit." Working the dark soft soil with his hands was what Ten loved most about farming, especially when the earth was deep and rich. He hoped the little ones would come to feel the same way. All the children nodded politely. They thought they already knew what to do. "What is there to learn?" thought 9-year-old Margaret, "All you do is drop the seed in the dirt and water it." She didn't dare say that out loud.

Early spring was the time of year Lottie cleaned the house. Dirt and soot had settled in during the cold winter days. As soon as the sun began warming the afternoon air, she did her best to get a head start on spring cleaning before planting hit. She had to finish one project first and before beginning another. It was hard for her to get it all done simultaneously, all while feeding the family and watching the kids. She hauled out blankets, bedding, pillows, and her treasured rug, setting them one by one against the fence and beating them with a big flat racket. Dust billowed out with each beat. Spitting dust out of her mouth, she frequently swiped the hair out of her face trying to brush away the dirt as well. Then, she worked on the timber-burning stove and fireplace. Before taking rugs back in, she hauled out the furniture to wipe the soot off the walls inside.

The girls helped with each step. Thankful for her wooden floor, she scrubbed it clean. Wils had installed the planks after their first winter. It had gotten so muddy that first winter, as the family tracked in snow and rain, Wils promised to put in a new floor that following summer. Ten had watched Lottie during all this time and tried to recall years past when she easily did all this work. He remembered her to be so strong and full of energy. Did she run out of breath so quickly back then, or was it his imagination that she seemed so exhausted at the end of each day?

The effort to get the house ready before taking on spring planting took more than a week of days. Finally, Lottie was prepared to bring items back inside. She collapsed in her kitchen and smelled the clean air; glad the spring cleaning was complete until next year.

Abraham Lincoln Assassinated

It was Wednesday, April 17, 1865, a week after Easter. Ten will never forget that date. They had nearly finished planting the starters for broccoli, carrots, and peas; and he'd finished an inventory of seeds stored in the cellar as he planned May and June planting. Hoping to have a substantial yield this year, he wanted additional seed supply. He hitched Smokey to the wagon. The ride into town and change of scenery would be a treat. It was a pleasant day, and he listened to the birds sing as he checked out the status of the neighbor's fields. He rode up to the general store in town, and jumped off the wagon, throwing the reins over the post. Folks were in town, but they were gathered in small groups, agitated and whispering loudly. As he stepped into the general store, he hollered, "Hey Les, how're ya?" Les did not respond. Ten hesitated and asked, "What's going on?" He saw Les helping someone at the register. The two men had very somber looks on their faces.

"Hey Ten." Les replied as he looked up without a smile. "The paper just got a telegram this morning; Lincoln was shot dead. Last Saturday night. The night before Easter," Les paused a moment, "He's dead, Ten!"

Ten was stunned. "What?"

"Some guy snuck into the theater and shot him in the head." Les replied. "The whole town is in shock. We don't know what it means." Les was worried, "We're all wondering, what happens now? Will the country collapse?"

"I hope not." Ten replied. He stared at the two men. No one had anything more to say. Les looked back and completed his transaction. Wordlessly, Ten went about his purchases and checked out. "Thanks," Les said as Ten nodded, turned, and headed out.

Outside, he loaded up the wagon. As he turned to climb on the wagon, he almost fell backward as his night visitor flashed before his eyes. He swayed, shook his head as he tried to regain his balance. He looked around to see if anyone noticed. A family down by the livery was watching him. He knew them from church but had never spoken to them. He saw two young boys loading the wagon and a young girl holding the little ones close to her side as they watched him. "I think that's the Rogers family from church." Ten spoke to himself. "Hope they don't think I'm crazy." Tossing that thought, he hopped up on the wagon and headed back out of town. "I need to tell Wils and Lottie what's happened!"

They were shocked to hear the news. "Whatever will happen now? What is to become of us? Will life ever be the same?" Lottie asked. They decided to make a better effort to keep in touch regularly with town folk. Lottie took the wagon over to the pastor's house to see if the church knew anything. James, the telegraph operator, promised to hang flyers with updates on his front door, and keep the church updated. The pastor posted those updates on his front door, and he promised to provide the newest information every Sunday at the beginning of church service. From there, the members would decide if anything needed to be done.

Wils commented, "I guess they've already sworn Andrew Johnson in as president. Imagine that. We already have a new president! And we didn't even know it was happening."

Ten stood up with a deep sigh; he was jittery and needed to move. "We got to put in the potatoes. Now is a good time as any to get started while we still have evening light. Duke, come with me, I'll show you how to dig the trench." As they headed out, Ten decided he would go into town this next week and see what more news he could discover.

Lottie had already brought the seed potatoes up from the cellar and showed the girls how to cut them, two eyes per section. The prepared seed potatoes were out back of the house, waiting for planting. They planned to plant the potatoes in the field nearest the house. Ten picked up a tray and nodded to Duke to take the other. Using this field would help Lottie keep an eye on the sprouts, weeds, and thinning tasks. She could then send Duke out to work the thinning as needed.

Ten explained as he started digging, "You gotta start with a trench about the depth of your foot. The width of my hand at the top and maybe half that at the bottom." Ten finished the first length while Duke watched and shaped the trench. Duke dug the second trench and began to enjoy digging in the soft black dirt to see how fast he could go. Ten went to get the rest of the seed potatoes. As Ten returned, he saw Duke's trench work veering way off track from the first trench. "Whoa! "Ten hollered, "where are you going? You'll end up in town if you go off that way. You've got to run parallel lines! "

Duke stopped and looked at Ten, "Parallel lines?" and then looked back at his trench. Sure enough, it looked like he was bending to the left. He looked sheepishly at Ten and both laughed. Kicking the dirt back into the trench, Ten laughed, "Well, looks like we gotta start over. I'll show you, real quick, how to keep a straight line. But it's getting dark, so we'll have you do a quick run of it and then give it another try in the morning." Ten showed him how to use a tree in the distance as a marker to keep his lines straight. Duke kept an eye just above his spade as he dug the trench again. The ache in his arms grew. He didn't stop, but his pace slowed down. Ten was beginning to think they wouldn't get the planting done in time to go see his pa.

Anxious, he started setting in a few seed potatoes in the first trench. When Duke completed the trench, Ten showed him how to set the potatoes. After a few sets, Duke had it down, and they stopped for the night. The next morning, Ten continued with the trenching to speed things up, thankful Duke was better at putting in the seed potatoes.

Most of the time, the chickens had to fend for themselves, eating what bugs and seeds they could find. Making sure they did get food, the girls often tended to the chickens by tossing grain, scraps, and waste from the kitchen. In the evening, after dinner, the girls would shoo them into the barn. When Lottie identified the next chicken destined for the pot, she told the girls to fatten that one up with table scraps. That message usually meant the hen was no longer laying eggs.

On Tuesday Ten broke away from chores to ride into town hoping, to hear news of the war. He hopped off the wagon and headed inside the general store, but he paused as he heard yelling from the livery. Les looked up startled and then relaxed when he saw Ten. "Oh, hi Ten. How are you?"

"Seems there is always something happening when I come to town. What's going on at Gus's livery?"

"There is some crazy guy down there." Les replied, "He came in last night and he's been ranting ever since!"

Ten frowned and asked, "Where's the sheriff?"

"He went to Joliet on some kind of training for confederate rebels; due back Thursday."

Ten turned around, went to the wagon, and grabbed his rifle. Les called after him, "Ten, you be careful."

"I'm fine, Les. I was trained for this kind of thing, remember?" Ten thought to himself, "Well, kind of trained..."

A Soldier's Dream, 1864

Ten walked on down to the livery and hesitated outside the open doors. He could hear a man yelling about his horse being stolen. He could hear Ol' Gus, the livery owner, yelling back, "I don't have your horse. These are all regular boards." The man wasn't listening to Ol' Gus. Peeking inside, he saw Ol' Gus in a stall with his hands in the air. The stranger had his back to Ten and was yelling at Gus. Ten waited silently for a moment. When the man stopped to catch a breath, he stepped in and cocked his rifle. Hoping the sound of the rifle would be enough, Ten waited a moment before speaking. "Now mister, I've shot a man and watched a man die. I've done it before and can do it again. So, you just drop that gun and slowly turn around."

The man dropped the gun and turned slowly. Gus scrambled around the man, grabbed the gun, and aimed it. Ten waited until Ol' Gus braced himself, his eyes going from Gus back to the stranger.

The stranger looked at Ten and asked, "You in the war?"

Ten responded maintaining a grim tone, "Yes."

"Union Army?"

"Yes. You?"

The stranger replied, "Yes, I just got out and can't find my way home. That horse is all I have and now I can't find it." He sank to the ground and sobbed.

Both Gus and Ten were surprised at the man's collapse. Ten thought a moment. "Now mister, I tell you what. We are going to walk you over to the jail house. You will have a nice bed, food, water, and even a bedpan. It will be nicer than the army gave you. I promise. You can stay there til the sheriff gets back and he will help you find your horse."

To Ten's surprise, the man was not so crazy to resist and walked calmly over to the jailhouse. Ol' Gus found the keys in the sheriff's desk and locked the man in a cell. "The ladies at the boarding house take care of prisoners. I'll let them know they have a 'guest.' Gus emphasized the word guest.

Ten thanked Gus and turned back towards the general store. Les was standing outside his door, watching. He backed into the store as Ten came up. "Wow, that was impressive, Ten."

"Aw, Les, like I said, the army trains you for that kind of stuff." Ten replied. "I think I'll head back home; too much excitement here for me."

"What did you need Ten?" Les asked.

"Nothing that can't wait." And Ten jumped up on the wagon and turned back the way he rode in. He didn't mention the event to either Wils or Lottie.

It was April 30 before they heard any update on the assassination. On Sunday morning, the pastor announced, "I'm happy to announce the assassination suspect, John Wilkes Booth, was surrounded in a barn, shot and killed last Wednesday. Turns out he was an actor and knew his way around the theater. He was even wearing a disguise!" The pastor paused and bowed his head, "May God forgive him for his terrible deed, and Lord, please bless our country in the stormy days that continue. Give us strength and determination to rebuild our land in peace. Amen." The congregation gave an obligatory "Amen," knowing that's how they should feel, but many told themselves they would need to work on forgiveness.

After the service, the congregation was preparing a potluck lunch. Lottie was at the food table setting out food when the woman from the boarding house slipped up to Lottie and told her what happened at Gus's livery. "What!" Lottie exclaimed as she looked over at Ten. She saw Wils, Les and several other men surrounding Ten.

Les had already told most of the town folk. The farmers hadn't heard so Les was thrilled to share it again. "Ten just walked right on down there without a second thought."

Ten wanted to change the subject, "Les, did the sheriff get back?"

"Yes, he got back Thursday and spent time with the man on Friday. Turned out the man had fought in the war and was trying to get home. He was lost, and all he had left was his horse. He figured out the man did have a horse, but he thinks it ran off. Sheriff offered to take him out and help look for it, if he promised never to come back to town."

Another man interrupted, "I saw the sheriff ride back in town after taking that. He was alone. I just assumed they found the horse."

On the return home, the children in the wagon wanted Ten to tell them the story again. Lottie and Wils were all ears. "Y'all heard it already, not much else to say." Ten was sorry he had ridden in with the family this week. He preferred to ride Smokey so he could slip out. But Lottie asked that he ride in the wagon with the family.

Lottie looked around at Duke, "Now don't you get any ideas." Duke knew not to respond.

Lottie knew Ten was uncomfortable and changed the subject for him, "Well, I'm glad they got Booth. We need to be one country again. This killing needs to stop before our boys come of age. I don't want them to see what Ten has seen." She stopped suddenly and looked over at Ten hoping she hadn't offended him. They had never told Ten they could hear him cry out at night.

He looked back at her and smiled, "I understand Lottie, I don't want them to see it either!"

Wils changed the subject, "Some folks are misguided, and a few are downright bad. Booth was a bad mad man. You'll know right away when you see it. Duke, just turn and walk away. Not worth the trouble they bring." Again, Duke said nothing.

These were busy days. They carefully seeded beets, peas, carrots, and kale. Duke learning every step of the way. They'd never planted this much before. All of these first crops would be ready to harvest at the end of June, early July. As soon as they finished the first planting the first crops, Ten turned to the large gentle slopes to work the corn and beans. He intended to provide a staggered timeline for planting and harvesting one crop after another. Ten taught Duke to check the fencing, gates, corrals, barn and other enclosures to ensure they were secure and solid. He explained that this would be important when the heavy thunderstorms arrive during the summer. "You'll understand in the next few months." Ten assured Duke as he showed the boy how to straighten and secure a leaning fence post.

Wilson built the finest equipment available. The cultivator was a two-horse piece of equipment, and Ten planned to use both Smokey and Wilson's horse. To get the horses familiar with the cultivator, he started with one horse at a time and just walked around a bit. It felt a bit like a wagon and both horses settled in quite nicely. It was time to hitch them both to the cultivator. Soon Ten was in the fields turning the soil.

Ten was amazed at how well the new cultivator turned the soil, it was so much faster. This equipment was new to him, so he did it himself for the first couple acres. Once he knew how to operate the equipment then he could teach Duke. Not until then would he hand over the reins.

In the field he just cleared, the tree trunks were still in place, and it would take another year before he could begin to clear those out. He needed to let the trunks rot a bit first. But after planting the other fields, he planned to plow around those trunks to help air and water seep in the soil and get it ready for future planting.

Ten was amazed at how well the new cultivator turned the soil, it was so much faster. This equipment was new to him, so he did it himself for the first couple acres. Once he knew how to operate the equipment then he could teach Duke. Not until then would he hand over the reins.

In the field he just cleared, the tree trunks were still in place, and it would take another year before he could begin to clear those out. He needed to let the trunks rot a bit first. But after planting the other fields, he planned to plow around those trunks to help air and water seep in the soil and get it ready for future planting.

He showed Duke what to do and often sent him back to repeat his work. Ten was meticulous and regularly reminded Duke how to till the soil and set it up for seed. Ten knew Duke could do it. Watching the young boy closely, Ten would correct him with 'do over' instructions. "When you turn the soil, you can't miss a spot. You can't leave big clods of soil. The young sprouts won't be able to get around it and will go to waste. We can't afford that." Or, "The cornrows can't be too high, and the seed can't go too deep. Plant it just to your middle knuckle. That gives room for the plant to create a solid cone at the base. That cone will support the stalk as it grows. Remember if you are going to do a job, do it well, or not at all." Ten thought to himself and added, "Also, people will be watching your fields to see how good a farmer you are." He smiled as he watched Duke head back out to work the missed spots, thinking to himself, "I sound like my Pa!"

He shifted to a rotary spader for last year's fields, and turning that soil went much faster than he had anticipated. He was glad to have Duke follow from behind, working in the manure and compost before planting. He was amazed at the progress of science in farming over a few short years. How much easier it was these days. But he kept hearing in town that big business with fancy machinery was taking over more farms. The competition was going to be intense when selling their produce. Luckily, Wils had built this equipment. He used the plans and profits from his work to develop his own machinery. Ten found it helped them compete with the big farmers. With these tools, they were able to increase their yield, harvest faster and get it in more quickly.

Ten's uninvited guest, Michael, settled down during planting season. At least during the day. The visions still came nightly, but they didn't seem as vivid. Ten was happy in the fields. He loved experimenting with the new equipment and planning the planting and training Duke occupied his mind. Nights were a different story. Ten dreaded going to sleep. In the beginning, he spent evenings with the family until sheer exhaustion forced him back to the bunkhouse. At times he sensed he'd stayed too long and that Lottie and Wils wanted him to leave. They were too polite to say anything. Once he caught on, he decided to occupy himself in the bunkhouse more often. After supper, he would rise and come up with a reason to leave, "Thanks Lottie, that was a fine meal. If you don't mind, I need to repair that harness for Smokey." Lottie and Wils smiled and seemed grateful as Ten headed out.

He stopped at the barn to see Smokey. Ten began to stop in the barn every night to spend time grooming Smokey. The days were long, and it was good for them to have quiet time together. It helped Ten shift his mind to peaceful thoughts before heading to bed.

During the summer, seemingly little chores were constant. The children were able to help. Bugs were a continuous battle. Both Ten and Lottie taught the children to search for bugs and destroy them. The minute the children seemed bored; Lottie would send them out to hunt bugs. They learned to smear the aphids on the leaves, and pick beetles and worms from leaves, put them in a bucket, and toss them into

Wils fire back at the blacksmith shed. Everyone pulled weeds continuously. Some required digging. Every day Lottie sent someone out to pull weeds, hunt and kill bugs. Ten continued to coach Duke on larger jobs, clearing out dead timber, cutting it into firewood, all the while explaining these were things he could do while Ten was gone to see his pa

Not all predators were bugs. Ten and the children knew to watch for scat from coyotes and cougars. Wolves were gone now, but there was one type of scat the children had not yet seen. Ten saw it as they headed out one morning to pull weeds and check the seedlings. Bear scat! Bears had wandered into the area, were hungry, and hunting for food. He stopped short, pointing out the pile of scat. "See that, kids?" as he pointed to the scat. "This is fresh scat from a bear. We need to keep an eye out. I'm hoping it's a male; we don't want a momma with cubs on our hands." The children were wide-eyed with excitement. Duke held on tight to his rifle and started looking into the trees surrounding the field. "You all need to stay close to Duke and me, but keep making a lot of noise, we don't want to surprise anything that could be out there. They should leave us alone."

Margaret shouted, "Let's sing 'Listen to the Mockingbird'!" And she broke out with the chorus,

"Listen to the mockingbird, listen to the mockingbird. The mockingbird still singing o'er the grave. Listen to the mockingbird..." The rest chimed in and skipped around Duke and Ten. The family laughed and continued toward the fields.

It wasn't long before Ten heard a grunt in the distance. He stopped and looked intently into the trees. He thought it was a bear digging into the trunk of a tree. Ten looked at Duke and tipped his head toward the tree. Margaret stopped singing as she saw the two men stop and stare into the trees. The others followed suit. The bear had already spotted them and had pulled away from the tree. Standing on its legs, it swayed back and forth, trying to catch their scent. "It's a male." Ten said quietly, "Everyone cluster close and stand tall. Look big!" Ten said quietly. The bear quit swaying, turned to the left, and hesitated a moment. It dropped on all fours and strolled away. Ten held his hand spread out, cueing everyone to keep still. "He's leaving. We will wait here a while, and I'll take you all back to the house."

When they got close to the yard, the children burst into a run and dashed straight into the kitchen. "Mama, Mama! We saw a bear!" Lottie turned around and looked at Ten and Duke wide-eyed.

"A bear? It's been so long since we've seen one around here!"

"Yea, I think he was passing through, found a beehive and was having a good meal. He wasn't interested in us. He headed on down toward the creek, I guess. He will follow along the creek for a while. Good fish there."

Easy days for Lottie were laundry days. She carried soiled clothing out to the pond, and the girls came along. As Lottie scrubbed on a washboard, the girls would wring out excess water and pile the clothing in a basket. They would each carry a basket to the back yard of house where Lottie would hang items to dry. Doing the laundry usually took several days. Once that was completed, she would resort to canning and preparing dinners. She was always grateful for fresh meat or eggs. It made a tasty dinner so easy. Otherwise, they resorted to soups and jerky. Jerky needed to be dried during the hottest days of the summer. But it would last all winter. She had gotten pretty good at estimating how much to make. But usually, by spring, the supply of jerky could get scarce.

July brought sizzle and drizzle. It was hot, and the rain came almost daily. It was difficult getting out to manage the crops, hoe the garden and clear the bugs.

Thankfully, they were inevitably covered in mud at the end of the day. Sometimes they slathered mud over their arms, face and legs as protection from bugs and the hot sun.

One morning Ten spotted a thistle just starting up. He gathered all the children, "See this? You know those tall purple flowers we fight all the time? This is what it looks like when it starts." He bent down and pulled it up with the roots. "We must never let these grow. If we get them when they are tiny like this, it's easy. Otherwise, we end up with a shovel and digging like crazy and burning the blossoms."

Finding a dry day to put up the hay was difficult. Ten, also, kept a close eye on the corn. When it drizzled, Ten coached the boy, "Okay Duke, now is when we mulch and thin the corn. You must do this when it is about five inches tall. Keep an eye on this. Don't count on your ma to do it for you. I need your help, as I am busy with setting out plants for the fall garden." Duke groaned, thinking, "It doesn't end!" But he knew not to say anything. He had come to respect Ten's knowledge, especially after the incident at the livery stable in town. Ten went on, "Oh, and be sure to keep an eye on the weeds; we can't let them go to seed! That means you need to walk the rows every day. Bring the little ones and take the hoe with you."

July also brought cherries and apples! The girls picked cherries off the tree and spent the afternoon pitting cherries in the backyard. Cherry juice squirted all over their dresses, pigtails, hands and faces. Once pitted, Lottie sent them down to the pond to wash off and rinse their clothes. The children giggled with glee as they pitted the cherries, knowing cherry pie would soon be on the table. The family loved cherry pie.

Late July brought a stormy morning. Ten had planned on getting the animals ready for a full day of work in the fields. But he delayed when he saw the stormy skies; he stayed inside the barn to clean, hoping things would clear up. He asked Lottie and the girls to be sure and tend to the garden right away before the rain started. The goats kept an eye on Ten as he moved through the barn. Finished, he headed out of the barn and studied the sky. Dark clouds were rolling in. The silence in the air was heavy. The clouds piled up with a furor, and silent lightning flashed in the distance.

"Whoa, this is gonna to be a big one." He ran to the house to warn the family. Wils was already at work in the blacksmith shop trying to get some firing done before the afternoon heat set in. "Hey, we got a storm brewing. Come on out! We need to batten up

the barn and make sure all the animals are secure!"
Ten had already worked out the chores for each
member of the family in storms like this. The plan
was to ensure the livestock were let loose in the large
pasture up the hill by the tall elm tree, which would
serve as cover. Ten managed that task. If the winds
damaged the barn, they didn't want any animals
stuck inside or injured. It was safer outside. Duke
brought the heavier farm equipment into the barn.
The younger children were to gather smaller animals,
chickens, and goats into the shed beside the house.
They hoped the house would provide adequate
protection for the shed.

Once preparations were complete, they counted all
the animals. The girls and Lottie counted chickens
and goats in the shed to ensure they'd gathered all of
them. Wils and Ten did a final count of the livestock
in the field. Finally, the family came back into the
house. Ten grabbed some food and water, waved
goodbye, and headed to the bunkhouse. The winds
blew hard, and the rain pelted the Fierce farm.
Lightning flashed, and thunder roared throughout the
day. Ten was grateful this storm was arriving in the
morning, hoping it would clear this afternoon and he
could check on storm damage in daylight. In
addition, those lightning flashes could cause him all
kinds of problems in the night, triggering his visitor

to flare up. Today, he sat on his bed, mending harnesses, sharpening, and oiling tools.

The storm began to let up late afternoon, and Ten was encouraged when the wind died down, and the thunder faded into the distance. He peeked out the door and saw flooding in the lower bean field. "That field drains nicely, so maybe the plants will survive." he thought. He glanced up the hill where the livestock stood. In the distance, he could see a good number of cattle. "Well looks like most of them are still okay." He looked harder to be sure Smokey was there. It took a few moments, but he finally spotted Smokey on the far side of the herd. Ten smiled and pulled his head back inside. He sat down and put on his boots, getting ready to slosh through the mud for a closer check.

Lottie and the children knew their jobs after the storm, were to clean up loose debris and count the small livestock as they let them out of the shed. The children tumbled out of the house, excited to see what had happened. Lottie put them to work immediately. Ten headed up the hill. Stormy came up to greet him right away and followed him as he wandered the field checking the cows. He saw some blood on one cow and headed over to it. As Ten walked around, he saw lots of blood and a big gash on its side. He looked around and saw a large tree branch about 20 feet away. "Ah," Ten thought. "She got hit by a tree branch. Gotta stop the bleeding." He pushed the wound closed with his fingers, took off his shirt, folded it, and laid it gently over the closed wound. Slight pressure would help stop the bleeding. The cow stirred but allowed Ten to stand there. As Wils inspected his blacksmith shop, he noticed Ten standing next to the cow for quite a while. Concerned, he came on up to see what was happening. "Wils, can you get me some clean water? As soon as I get this to stop bleeding, I'd like to wash it out."

Wils turned around and said, "Sure." He ran back and carried back two buckets of water, Duke followed with two more buckets and a rope. Ten slowly and carefully poured the water over the wound. They fashioned a noose around the cow and led it back down to the corral. "Let's keep him in here for a while and watch the wound, so it doesn't get infected. We can run water over it each day." This reminded him of tending wounded troops after a skirmish. He saw plenty of that during the war and wished he had the gear to stitch the cow's wounds.

Ten stood up after cleaning the wound and looked at Duke, "You keep an eye on this one. I saw some cattle in the distance downhill. We are missing three." Ten jumped up on Smokey's bare back and continued, "Wind must have pushed them along. Smokey and I will go get them and bring them back."

Chapter 3

Saying Goodbye

It seemed forever, but finally, it was the end of July, and Ten was ready to take his pa to the Veteran's hospital in Rockford. Every evening for a week before leaving, Ten worked on the wagon, putting on a cover with bedding for Pa. He picked up a canvas in town and built a frame. Thankfully it had solid side panels to hold whatever cargo he would be carrying. Finally, the weather was mild and sunny, and there were no signs of storm in sight. Ten hoped to make the trip without any trouble.

Lottie helped him tie the canvas to the frame. She brought out old bedding the family had used over the winter and set them inside the wagon. Not sure if it would come back, Lottie told herself to set aside time this fall to make new bedding. She laid it out nicely for her pa. She had used all her scraps from old clothes to make the quilt. With the work Ten had done, Lottie was sure they would have a good crop, and perhaps she could afford to buy some fabric to make new clothing.

As he loaded up the wagon with supplies, Lottie brought out some of the canned beans from last year and tucked it in the back among the bedding. It was time. Smokey was looking forward to a ride. It had been a long time and pulling that cultivator back and forth in field rows was boring.

Lottie stepped back and put her hands on her hips and smiled. "Now, you just take care of Pa. We can cover things here if you need extra time." She waved as he started to pull away.

"Tell Wils not to burn himself!" Ten nodded towards the blacksmith's shop and smiled as he rode away.

It was noon on June 30th. Ten hoped to get to Persifer by late afternoon, August 1. It would have to be a short night, but he didn't sleep much these days anyway. Walnut Creek was about the halfway point, and he planned to camp there. He would have preferred not sleeping to avoid Michael's bloody visits, but he knew Smokey would need a break.

August 1865

He arrived in Persifer August 1. He decided to camp out on the edge of town, not wanting to bother Jane, his stepmother, and the children. As usual these days, Ten was awake as the first birds began to sing. He gathered his things, hitched Smokey, and checked the wagon to be sure it was ready to haul his pa to Rockford. It would be a three-day ride, so he was grateful for the cover over the wagon.

When Ten rode up, he could tell Jane had been watching for him. She came out to greet him before he had gotten off the wagon. "Hi Ten, I have to thank you for taking him up. He seems worse. You need to look at him." Ten hopped off the wagon and headed inside. "I fed your Pa what little he could eat and cleaned him up. I've done that every morning not knowing which day you might show up." She paused, "He's ready to go."

Ten dreaded getting his pa to the wagon. Jane was kind enough to let him take the bedding Simeon had been using and some extra blankets. Extra bedding would make it softer. Ten rolled up the bedding, took it out to the wagon, and fluffed it to make it more comfortable for his pa. Ten thought to himself, "Pa will have a good bed with both Jane's and Lottie's bedding to lie on." He quickly returned inside and heard Jane whispering to Simeon. "I'm sorry it worked out this way, Simeon. We could have had a good life." Jane almost seemed teary. "You will be better cared for at this hospital." Ten intentionally stumbled as he walked into the room, and Jane jumped onto her feet.

"I'm ready," Ten looked at his Pa. Simeon smiled meekly. Simeon winced as Jane and Ten each took an arm to help Simeon off the bed and sat him in a straight-backed wooden chair. It was painful every time he moved his leg.

Ten and Jane carried Simeon out to the wagon. They set the chair beside the back of the wagon, and all Simeon needed to do was stand. Ten climbed into the wagon, shimmied behind Simeon, put his forearms under Simeon's armpits, and lifted. Jane slipped her arms under his knees. They lifted him over to the back end of the wagon. Simeon groaned as he slowly sat on to the bedding. "Hey this is nice and soft," Simeon smiled weakly. Ten stepped further back and helped his pa lay down. Ten had to crouch as there was not much headroom under the canvas. Simeon groaned quietly with each movement.

Ten knew his pa was doing his best not to complain, "Pa, it will be a slow ride. We can stop as often as you want. We might even ride into the night as long as you can take it. Smokey will need a break, but I don't need to sleep much these days." Ten thought of his night visitor. "Just holler if you need anything, and I'll stop."

Jane put a bag of Simeon's things beside him and kissed him goodbye. She turned and headed back into the house.

As Ten and Simeon rode off, Jane hollered out, "Let me know how it goes."

Ten never planned on coming back through Persifer. Not sure if she could hear his response, he spoke, "Okay, I'm sure the hospital will let you know."

"You ready Pa?" Ten asked as his pa nodded.

"I'm ready," he said. "What route are you taking?"

"I think I'll head north to Green River and camp there. Then up to Rock River. We'll follow it to Rockford. It will take a couple of nights but should be pretty easy." Ten climbed up on the wagon, took the reins, and flicked them. "Let's go, Smokey." He slowly rolled the wagon out of town towards Rockford. It was 150 miles north, northeast. They rode in silence. The sun was warm on Ten's back in the cool air. Ten was grateful for the sun, knowing it help Simeon keep warm inside the wagon. They rode for hours. Tedium. Ten was thankful for tedium. It was predictable. The rolling of the wagon brought a rocking peace. But if he wasn't careful, if he let his mind rest, Michael could show up.

Ten let Smokey pull the wagon along the dirt road. While they rambled slowly along the road, he directed his recollections back to his childhood. By controlling his thoughts, he effectively kept Michael suppressed, so Ten had become quite good at managing quiet time with directing his thinking. He discovered there were many things he could ponder. His first thoughts were about his mother. He still missed her. She'd had nine children before Ten was born and had worked hard to help Pa on the farm. Ten remembered, she seemed weak after John, his little brother, came along. Ten suddenly thought of Lottie. "Interesting," he said quietly to himself. "Lottie has that same weary look bout her." Ten went back to thoughts of his mother. She was so ill in the end; Ten remembered hearing the doctor explain she had consumption and was having trouble fighting it. At the time, Ten had no idea what that meant. During her last days, she stayed in her room, and only Pa went in to feed her. Ten watched Pa forget about farming, the animals, everything, as he tried to care for her. It was fall of 1858, and the older siblings had already left home. Ten helped as he could, bringing in the harvest, managing the livestock, and watching his little brother, John. He found himself alone in the fields, helplessly racing against the clock as he watched the crops rot while his mother, Samantha, faded away in her room, Simeon at her side. Income from the harvest that year was not good, and Simeon could not pay taxes on the property. The state had already taken the Vermillion County farmland Simeon had first purchased on the east side of Illinois.

Ten continued reminiscing. "Lottie married well. Wils makes a fine living and sure knows how to design and make new equipment. It's the edge a farmer needs to survive these days. So much has changed since Ma died."

"And that's when Wils stepped in." remembered Ten. "I will always remember Wils help after Ma died. He said he needed us, but really, he was just helping us out." Ten remembered those first days at the Fierce household when he and his brother tried their best to work Wils land. "Wils was smart to be a blacksmith." Ten thought to himself, "Work is booming for him now, and this time, he needs me. These big farmers want all kinds of new equipment ... and that new plow he's making for Frank is great. He's making single and multiple plows! And I get to use the ones he builds for us."

Ten's thoughts turned to his sister, Phietta, alone with all her children. He wondered what happened to Sam. Ten was glad Wils offered a place for her. He missed family and wondered if she would come to stay with them soon.

"Ten?" Pa called to his son.

"Ah, at least he's awake." Ten thought, "Yea, Pa."

"I need a break, can we stop?" Ten checked the sun, it must have been several hours. The sun was straight overhead. Pa was right; it was time for a break and some food.

"Sure, Pa, let me find a place to pull over." The two men didn't talk much. Pa stayed in the wagon. Ten tried to get him to take some water or broth. Simeon wasn't interested. He just needed the motion of the rolling wagon to stop for a while. Ten gave Smokey some water and sat down to eat the beans and dried pork Lottie had given him. "We'll go a little further; the river isn't very far now. We can stop there for the night."

Ten rode 'til the sun hung low in the west. When he heard the ripples of the Green River lapping along the shoreline, he began looking for a spot to set camp. It wasn't long; he spotted a place near the riverbank for the night. Ten unhitched Smokey and let him loose to drink and graze on the grass. He built a fire and sat down to eat. "Hey, Ten," Simeon called out.

"Yea, Pa. You okay?"

"Actually, not bad. I could get out and take a leak. Can you help?"

Jane had given Ten a jar for this purpose. He brought the jar to his Pa and helped Simeon sit up. After doing his business, Simeon laid back down. Rolling back and forth in constant motion was fatiguing. Jane had sent a chair along, but he wasn't up to sitting in a chair. Ten reached down and picked up a long narrow stick, dropped the backboard down and sat on it with his feet dangling. He began to draw in the dirt.

Simeon asked, "How are you?"

"I'm fine. Glad to take a break. Pa, did you know? Someone killed Lincoln last Easter?"

"Oh no." Simeon groaned. "He was a good man. What happens now?"

Ten responded, "They tried but didn't kill anybody else, just Lincoln. Then... well, Andrew Johnson was sworn in as President the very next day. Smooth as anythin'. General Lee surrendered a week before, and we all thought that was it was over. But it took 'til June for the rest of the Confederate Generals to finally succumb."

Simeon interrupted, "What can Johnson do? He seems weak to me."

Ten went on, "I dunno, I hear there's still a lot of Southern resistance out there." Then, trying to move on from politics, Ten asked, "Tell me, Pa, how was it for you?"

Simeon knew what Ten was asking. He didn't like to talk about the war, but the two had it in common. But more importantly, they had shared so much in life already, and they could share their war stories, knowing the other would understand.

"You know Ten, I wanted to make a difference." He waited a bit to catch his breath. "I know I pushed my luck being so old. But they needed troops in so short a time they just didn't care." Simeon chuckled, then groaned, "I told them I was 47."

"But Pa, you were 61, a big difference!" Ten was looking down at the dirt below as he tapped the stick on the ground.

"I know, you told me that when I mustered in. When Lincoln called for us, they were desperate to end the war. I'd heard they were overlooking certain things. And they sure did with me. I knew I could pass the same test as any of them. Age was my problem. I easily mustered in. I was proud of that. I knew this was a chance to do my part."

"You were in the 39th, right Pa?" Ten asked.

"Yes," Simeon watched Ten frowning and poking the ground with his stick. "I named you after Grandfather Wareham. Let me tell you about him. He was a Lieutenant in the Revolutionary War; and fought many years for our country. As he got old, we would visit him, and he told us so many stories."

Ten knew what was coming. Simeon told these stories many times, he continued, "One time he was at Fort Ticonderoga. He had to take sick soldiers down to Connecticut. He only had two days of provisions. Ten, all those men had to eat was four ounces of beef and one gill (1/2 cup) of rice a day. When they got to Fort George, there was no food for them. Not even salt. Captain Phelps understood the desperate situation these men were in and that they needed healthy soldiers. Captain Phelps gave Lt. Gibbs a loan, which got them to Albany. The Captain said he didn't have orders to give them money, and it could mean trouble from the General, but he took the risk anyway. Because of that Captain, they made it. In turn, your Great Grandfather sent a letter[vi] to Governor Trumbull to report the desperation of his sick soldiers and how Captain Phelps' helped. Your grandfather promised to be careful with supplies over the next year to make up for the loan."

Ten shook his head, remembering how scarce food was when he was serving just last summer, "I remember this story Pa, you told me about him when I was a kid. I always wondered how they could stay alive on that much food." Ten responded.

Simeon continued, "And it was only October; they still had a hard winter ahead of them. He took care of his men." Simeon went on with a weak voice, "I am proud to be his grandson.

Ten listened carefully, thankful for this time with his pa. He gazed at the dirt and started drawing a circle with his stick, "But Pa, you've been a good man all your life, you didn't need to muster in to prove it.

"I know Ten; this was something I had to do. Sure, it came late in life for me, but it was my moment to do what I could for my country, like Grandpa Wareham." Simeon paused to think, "Samantha was gone, y'all were grown up and could fend for yourselves. I couldn't stand by and do nothing, while the Confederates tear apart the country we worked so hard to create.

"I knew Abe Lincoln over in Vermillion County when he was just a lawyer. He is a good man, and I wanted to back him up." Simeon paused to take a breath and went on, "This is a free country. That was what Grandpa Wareham fought for, freedom. People should be free to come and go as they please. If you want to farm, there is plenty of land out west. That's what is so great about our country. Your Great Grandpa did his part, so when Lincoln called us up, I had to go."

Ten looked up, thinking about his own experience, "Pa, did you see much fighting?"

"Nah, I didn't see too much, just a skirmish here and there. But they kept moving us around. We marched 150 miles from Cumberland to Virginia. Then, after just one day's rest, we marched 150 some miles back to Cumberland. Then, we had to turn around and head back to Virginia again. We couldn't figure out why we were going back and forth. It didn't make much sense. We finally ended up at Harrison's Landing. That's when my age caught up with me; I couldn't keep up with the young guys. Most of us were sick and exhausted. We weren't in any condition to face the Confederates. That's when I got wounded. It was pretty early on in the skirmish. I don't remember much about it, I just suddenly found myself lying in the field. I didn't know what was hap'ning 'til the fighting was over." Simeon waited a moment, remembering lying there in the field, with a cloudy gray sky overhead, bleeding and in pain.

"At least they came and got me. But little difference it made; they had no medical care, no bandages, no water to clean my wound. It was a mess.

"We were all sick. That was the worst of it. The food was bad; it was dirty, we were dirty. We didn't have supplies to do anything. I think I'd be okay if I hadn't gotten sick. I could have fought this off. It just didn't turn out the way I'd hoped."

Ten listened. Simeon continued talking about the marches, the filth, and the lack of food. He'd made good friends but had not seen or heard from any of them since they had sent him home on disability. "I don't know what happened to any of them." Simeon said sadly.

There was a long pause. Simeon stirred slightly as he prepared to change the subject. His voice had a somber yet passionate tone, that Ten hadn't heard since before the war.

"Ten, my life was good in the beginning. I sold my land in Ohio and used the money to buy good farmland over in Vermillion County. I worked it, built a home for Samantha and you kids while you stayed back in Ohio. Then, when Sam married Phietta, he took her to Knox County. That was 100 miles away from Vermillion. Wils was fixin' to marry Lottie, and they were gonna go to Knox County too. I reckoned I'd better join 'em. My mistake was I never sold the Vermillion acres. I lost it all when I couldn't pay the taxes."

Ten thought to himself, "I don't think Pa knows Sam left Phietta." He considered letting him know and decided no need. He let Simeon go on.

"Ten, please forgive Jane. She did her best. We thought we could help each other out. But with me like this, she was overwhelmed. Who'd of thought I'd come back this way?" Simeon and Ten sat in silence a while. They both knew their time together as father and son was nearly over. Simeon felt a need to cover a lot in the short time they had left.

"Jane's a good woman. She knows I will always love your Ma. Your Ma and I had some great moments together. Memories of those moments with Samantha are all have left now. I have nothing but memories. You know, love doesn't go away when one dies. We just have to wait until we can be together again. The Good Lord named me Simeon, so I understand what it means to wait." Simeon paused and seemed lost in a memory. His eyes distant as a gentle smile peaked through his pained expression. Ten waited, letting him have the memory. In a moment, Simeon blinked his eyes as if to remember where he was, and he drifted back to the wagon and Ten.

"After your ma died, I felt old and tired. But I had to keep on living. Joining the war gave me a sense of purpose I thought I'd lost. My time is almost over now. I drift into dreams and memories most of the time, and Ten, God has shown me, your future is bright. I'm proud of you, Ten... and all my kids." Simeon thought awhile, and with a deep sigh, he spoke more slowly now, "Samantha did a good job with y'all. And now, I am ready to die. I will see her soon."

Simeon had talked a long time and needed to rest, "Thanks for taking me to Rockford. Now Jane can get on with her life." His words came more slowly now. "I will wait there for the Lord to take me. I am ready." Simeon's voice trailed off. Then he spoke, "Tell me what happened to you, son." Simeon was ready to listen for a while.

"You know Pa; I'm tired. Let's call it a night. We can talk tomorrow when we pitch camp again.

"That's a good idea." Simeon drifted off to sleep immediately.

Ten continued to sit there watching the stars, thinking about his father's story. "They shouldn't have let him in. He was too old!" Ten thought. "But then, Ma shouldn't have died either. Pa would have been okay." Ten shook his head slowly, "So many 'should ovs' and 'shouldn't ovs'." He could run through those thoughts all night if he let it. He stood up to push them out. "I guess Michael will visit tonight." Ten thought, hoping his Pa would sleep through any noises he made.

It had been a long day. Ten unrolled his bedding and lay near the fire, and slowly faded to sleep. The next thing he knew, a bright light flashed in his eyes as a young man's white face loomed before him with blue eyes wide open, jaw dropped in alarm. Suddenly the man's eyes turned red, with blood dripping down his cheeks like tears. He started laughing and instantly pulled away into darkness. "No!" Once again, Ten shouted as he sat up. Once again, his horse startled and took a step back. Although he expected them, Smokey was still surprised with these sudden screams from his master. Ten looked around and immediately knew where he was and the current mission he was on. He sat quietly under the stars, listening for his pa, hoping he hadn't heard. The breeze rustled the leaves of the trees, and an owl hooted. Stormy nodded and snorted as he watched Ten lay back down to sleep, hoping it would be just a 'one visit night.'

That morning Ten rose quietly just before sunrise as the first bird began to chirp. He rolled his bedding and slipped it onto the front of the wagon at his feet. He planned to get moving slowly before his dad woke. He gazed to the east watching the pink sky fade to blue as a gentle breeze pushed puffy white clouds across the horizon. "I hope that breeze keeps up the rest of the day. Yesterday was a warm. If not, I'll water Pa down when we get to the next river."

After a few hours, they came upon Rock River. It was gorged, as it had been a wet year. He hadn't yet heard a peep from his pa. Ten noticed deer tracks along the bank. "Well, we will probably interrupt their drinking spot tonight." He thought as he pulled up on the reins stopping under the canopy of a large Elm tree. "We'll stop here for a while." This river would lead them to Rockford. He heard his pa rustling in back, "Ten?"

"Yea Pa,"

"I need to take a leak."

As Ten handed him the jar and lifted him slightly, he wondered if Pa had waited until the wagon stopped before asking for the jar. It was a good time to stop, eat and drink. It must have been mid-morning by the sun, so Ten hoped to skip a noon break. He would just have to pace the rest stops based on how his pa was doing.

That night Ten found a nice spot to camp. The deer tracks were still along the riverbank. "Maybe we'll see 'em." Ten thought. Again, he took care of Smokey first and then started a fire near the wagon.

"How ya doing, Pa?" Ten asked, peeking into the wagon.

"I'm ok. Hurts a lot, but that proves I'm still alive. You know Ten, you do know I'm dying, right?"

Ten looked at his pa silently, not knowing what to say.

"Pa, I hate to see you this way." Ten responded quietly. "Maybe the hospital will help you get better."

"I don't think so, Ten. But it will be a better place to die than where I was." He waited a moment, "Ten, talk to me. I heard you last night."

Startled, Ten looked at his pa. "You heard." He said.

"Yes, was that a nightmare?"

Ten stepped over by the fire. The night was quiet, and Simeon could easily hear Ten.

"Pa, I wasn't in the army that long, all it took was one skirmish. Like you, I was so proud... at first. I could think fast and scramble fast. Our job was to defend our garrison while the action was back east. Because I was smaller than the others, I was fast and could dart around, in and through the bushes, to move us forward faster. The captain used me as we scouted for Confederates or bushwhackers. We had no major battle, but we did have skirmishes, mostly with the bushwhackers. For the most part, it was boring. Drill practice, patrolling." He paused, "Except for one time." Ten's voice faded. Simeon stayed silent. He sensed the tension in his son and knew a significant story was coming.

"I killed somebody, Pa." Ten spoke bluntly.

Simeon waited. He hurt, this time not because of his leg, but because of the pain his son suffered.

Ten continued in short sentences, "We were down in Columbus, Kentucky. We were scouting those bushwhackers. They always tried to sneak up. The kid was my age. Like I said, I'm small... fast and strong." Ten sat up a bit straighter, "Colonel McChesney said I had a quick mind and moved fast. That made me proud. Guess being so short, you know, I've always done double time to keep up with the guys. I always did."

Simeon nodded, remembering his son's efforts as a young boy.

"Anyway, I had my musket using shrubs and trees as cover. I scrambled from one bush to another. I kept an eye out for trouble. Scramble, shoot, reload and scramble again. It was all just practice. But that day. I was ahead of my regiment doing my dash and dart thing. I was feeling pretty good about it, and I... I didn't see anyone coming. Then, then... I heard something. I crouched behind a bush."

"Suddenly, there was this kid. I saw his head coming up over the hill. He was running. I could tell he was a bushwhacker 'cause I saw his musket next to him. I shouldn't have shot him, though. Like I said I have quick reflexes, I peeked out through the bush. He came on up over the bluff and there he was. I aimed and fired. He was probably 20 feet away, but I can still see him like he was inches away."

"I watched him die, Pa. I see it over and over every night in my dreams. Sometimes, if I'm not careful, I see him during the day." The words came rushing out. He'd never talked about this. "Pa, his face pops up in my dreams, and suddenly he turns all bloody. He stared at me as he died. I can't forget it." Telling the story brought the image back in full color. It was vivid in Ten's mind. He could see the kid so clearly as if he was there with them right now. Ten was silent as he remembered the vision.

Simeon waited a bit to see if Ten had anything more to say. "Ten?"

"Yea, Pa."

"I wish you'd never seen that. But it was war. It's what you had to do. It's what they trained you to do. You were supposed to shoot him."

"I know Pa, but it doesn't make things any easier." Ten was exhausted. "I don't remember anything after that. Other than we ran 'em off. Sometimes, I just don't want to go another day if... if I have to see him again..." his voice trailed off.

"Ten, you need to find your peace and move on. You have a whole life to live. You are young, smart and can have a good life. If you work for it." Simeon waited a moment, "Promise me you will try."

Ten was glad he'd told his story to Pa. Somehow, things felt a little better, and his Pa understood. "I will, Pa. I never told anyone this before. It helps."

After some silence, Ten could hear his Pa's breath start to come slow and easy. He was asleep. Ten thought, I should get some sleep, too. "Oh Lord, please don't let Michael come tonight. I need rest."

Ten's mind began to wander. He began to think of Michael. The horror of that day stood out over all the others. It was just weeks away from discharge when it happened, "If only...."

As he prepared to lay down, Ten heard a voice behind him, "Ten." Startled, he looked around. Lifting the tarp, Ten saw his pa deep asleep. Perhaps he'd said something in his sleep. Ten turned back around and watched the trees as he added timber to the fire. "Ten." He heard it again. Puzzled, Ten kept looking around. "I need to talk to you." He turned and looked under the tarp; again. Again, his pa was still asleep. He shook his head as if to throw the voice out of his mind. The night fell silent after that.

The next thing Ten knew, the early birds were chirping, announcing the arrival of a new day. His visitor did not come that night. That had not happened since it happened in Kentucky. He got up quietly and rolled out slowly so as not to disturb his pa. They began the last leg of their journey to Rockford. Following along the river, Ten listened to the leaves rustle in the gentle breeze pushing them northward. Birds were chirping, he saw rabbits dashing into the bushes, and deer lift their heads to gaze at them as they rolled by. "It's a beautiful place, this land," thought Ten.

They arrived in Rockford on the August 7th. It was late in the afternoon as they rode up to the hospital.[vii] Ten was shocked. It was just a house! And a small house at that." He began to think this was a mistake, "Can they really take care of Pa here?" He pulled up on the street in front of the house. He walked up to the door and took off his hat as a nurse opened the door. "Hi, I'm Ten Gibbs, and I brought my Pa, Simeon."

"Yes, we've been waiting for him." She was kind and leaned to the right to look behind Ten to see where Simeon might be.

Ten tipped his head, "He's in the back of the wagon. I set up a little tent for the ride."

"Looks like it worked for you. I'm Marietta. Let's go out and check on him."

She stepped past Ten and walked to the back of the wagon. "Simeon?" she said as she came close.

"Yes." Simeon said softly.

"I'm Marietta, and I will be taking care of you."

"Hi, Marietta, good to meet you." Simeon was a courteous man and did his best to maintain a proper greeting, and then he drifted back to sleep. He had rallied to savor time with Ten during the trip, but now he was exhausted.

Marietta looked at Ten as he came up to the wagon. "I will get some men and a board to carry him in. I have a bed waiting for him." She headed back into the house as Ten sat down on the end of the wagon, watching his father sleep.

Ten watched as the men came out and loaded his pa on the board. Simeon moaned and rolled his head from side to side as the men shifted him onto the board. Ten was silent as they carried his pa into the house. He recalled when his Simeon had said he felt old; Ten felt old now. His Ma was gone, and his Pa would soon be gone. If it weren't for WIls and Lottie, he would be alone. "I wonder what lies ahead. Will it get any better?"

Marietta came back to say goodbye to Ten. As she approached them, he asked, "But this is a house. Will they care for him here?"

She smiled, "Yes, we've been using all kinds of facilities to care for our soldiers. Most of us are volunteers, and many hospitals will specialize. Our specialty is gangrene. We can take good care of your father here."

Ten liked Marietta and understood the need to use resources available during a time of war. He nodded and stepped backward to Stormy. "I'd like to come back and visit one day."

Marietta smiled and nodded as Ten mounted his horse, thinking Ten's pa might not be here when 'one day' comes.

Chapter 4

The Hitchhiker

With great sadness, Ten left the house fearing he might never see his pa again. He began his two-day ride back home, headed toward Rock River, which would guide his first leg of the trip. He pondered his father's words as he rolled out of Rockford. "Pa was right. I didn't have a choice." He thought. "I was trained to do that." He glared at the road ahead of him, "But I killed him." He spent the next two hours suppressing Michael from rising into his thoughts. Ten tried to focus on the pleasant sounds and beauty of the countryside. As he came up to Rock River, he saw a hitchhiker along the side of the road, a tall, dark man who appeared very strong. Ten slowed and pulled over to offer a ride, thinking to himself, "He looks like a war veteran. I bet he fought in one of the Illinois regiments." He smiled at the hiker, pulled up on the reins, and stopped by the man, "Where you headed?"

"South," the man responded, "no particular place."

"Well, I can carry you about 100 miles."

"Great." The man threw his duffle in the back of the wagon and climbed aboard.

"Call me Ten." Ten nodded a greeting as he flicked the reins, and Smokey began to move forward.

"Michael." The man responded and nodded back.

Ten stole a quick look at the man and sat a moment before responding. "Michael, huh?"

"Yup"

"Were you in the war?" Ten asked.

"I've fought in plenty of wars." He responded.

Ten wondered about that response. "Odd." He thought. "No young man in this country has seen more than one war." Wondering if this guy was a world traveler, he asked. "You've seen the world?"

"You could say that." Michael responded.

They sat in silence a while. Rolling along Rock River, Ten was thankful for the summer breeze, birds, and an occasional deer to keep them company. As they neared Green River, the hitchhiker broke the silence and said, "Ten, I am not the Michael that haunts you at night."

"What?" Ten stiffened and sat straight up. His eyes opened wide, but he kept staring at a rise in the road ahead of them. Smokey continued to plod along.

"I'm not the guy that visits you at night." He repeated.

Ten didn't know how to respond. As they reached the crest of the hill, open fields provided a great view of the horizon and all that lay between them and the skyline. The sun was hanging low in the west. It was late, but Ten wanted to ride until midnight if Smokey was up for it. They would take it slow. It was a quiet evening as the wagon continued along the road. Ten thought it seemed so much more peaceful than when they had traveled this same road just this morning.

"Yeah, that guy in your dreams?"

Ten was uncomfortable and shifted his weight as he made a fruitless effort to rest his body. He took a deep sigh and relaxed his arms to push out the tension. He decided not to say a thing to this man. "I should never have picked this guy up." He thought.

"That's good, Ten, just relax." Michael paused, "That guy in your dreams? I need to tell you- his name is not Michael. *I'm* Michael."

Ten, still stunned, mustered up the nerve to ask, "What *is* this?" He was suspicious of this man. Had he been following him? Did he listen in when he talked to his pa? Ten thought to himself, "This is just weird. How does he know about Michael?"

"I've been working with a lot of men, like you, that fought in the war. I'm here to tell you about that guy you call Michael."

"No!" Ten thought, "don't listen to him."

Michael went on, "You need to know; he is fine. All is well with him. He knows you didn't want to kill him." Ten's eyes grew wide as he frowned and stared straight ahead. He flipped the reins, and the wagon kept rolling along the road as Smokey continued to pull. "Ten, you are a good man, and you have much to accomplish in your life." Again,

Ten did not respond. He shuddered, flicked the reins and sped up as if to get away from the conversation.

Ten was finally able to speak, "How do you know me, and how do you know my visitor?"

"It's a gift I have." The man said briefly. He'd had this question before. He wondered if he needed to go more slowly with these young soldiers. The Civil War had been a gory one, and so many of their friends and family had died. He had many to see these days. So many men were suffering.

"Ten, I spoke too soon." They continued to ride in silence. Ten considered how he might gracefully let this odd man off the wagon so he could finish his ride alone.

They rode in silence. Michael knew Ten needed time to think. As Ten calmed down, he found the courage to ask Michael another question. "So... why're you here?" he asked.

"I'm here to help. That visitor of yours is not what you think. It's not a ghost. It's a memory. You will always remember what happened, and you will always feel bad about it. But it's not a place to stay. You can't live life frozen in that place and time. Let it thaw. Let it fade. For now, live in the moment and consider the possibility of a new dream for tomorrow. You may not believe it now, but you do have a choice." Michael paused and watched Ten's reaction to his words. "Listen to your pa. You need to let it go. And I can tell you how."

Ten stared straight ahead, pondering this man's words.

"You are a good man Ten." Michael continued, "No man should feel good about killing another. Because you feel bad about what happened tells me of your goodness inside. I've watched you work hard to take care of your family, your pa, your little brother, Lottie, and Wils, even Smokey. You have a good life waiting for you. It may take a while. But first, you must know and believe the young man you shot... is okay. And you can be too. One day, you will be ready to send that visitor away. When that day comes, you will discover who you are and what you can give this world." He paused a long while, sighed deeply, and spoke. "Until then, that night visitor will continue."

It was late, and the stars were shining bright. Smokey was slowing down, and Ten realized they needed to stop. "I need to stop. Smokey needs a break."

"See there Ten, you know your animal, and when Smokey needs a break, and you do it."

Ten looked at the man, he even knew Smokey's name.

While Ten was unhitching Smokey and giving him food and water, Michael said he would find some food and disappeared in the nearby timber. He had no knife or gun. Ten first took care of Smokey and then pulled out his gear. By the time Ten had a fire going, Michael was back with a fat quail in hand. "That was quick!" commented Ten.

"Well," the mysterious man said, "It was just there, and I was able to catch it by surprise. I move quietly."

The two men moved without speaking, letting the crickets, frogs, and sounds of the night fill the silence. They cleaned the quail, skewered it on a stick and cooked it over the fire. After picking off every last piece of meat, Ten was ready to go to sleep. He had not rested well during the ride to the hospital. He had constantly been on alert, listening for his pa. Ten laid down and fell asleep instantly. Again, a second night without his visitor. As usual, the early morning bird woke Ten around 4 A.M. He opened his eyes and saw the strange man called Michael sitting on a log near the fire. It was as if he had never slept. "Did you get any sleep?" Ten asked.

"I don't sleep much. I prefer to look at the stars," was the reply.

Quietly the men cleared camp. They put out the fire and jumped on the wagon for the next leg of the trip. They rode quietly. Ten kept shifting his weight, he was uncomfortable with this strange man sitting beside him. Smokey seemed fine, ambling down the road with the wagon rolling behind him. "Why did I pick him up?" Ten thought to himself. "I don't understand what is going on."

"Ten," Michael broke the silence. "I know what I said yesterday sounds strange. Take your time to think about it." Ten didn't respond, so Michael went on, "I've got another visit to make up the road here. So, I think I'll hop off now. I want to thank you for the ride."

"Sure," responded Ten. He pulled up on the reins and brought the wagon to a stop. "You are an interesting man, Michael. But I will give it some thought. I'd be glad to get rid of these night visits."

Michael smiled and hopped off the wagon. He tipped his hat, turned away, and walked off the side of the road and up the hill. Ten sat and watched the man walk away. "Hey, Michael," he yelled as the man slipped out of sight. Ten jumped off the wagon and ran after him. When he reached the crest of the hill, Michael was nowhere to be seen.

He turned back, "This whole thing must have been my imagination. All these strange thoughts in my head since the war."

But the words of the hitchhiker called Michael kept coming back to him as he continued his journey home. It was an exciting idea to think this visitor might actually stop his visits. Suddenly he felt a wave of loneliness come over him. "I guess I really am alone now." He thought. "I have to shake this off and make something of myself. Like Pa said, I need to make a new life."

He looked at Smokey, "Hey Smokey; you'll come with me, whatever happens, right?" The horse bobbed its head and snorted as if in response. Ten began to think about the farm back at Wils and Lottie's place for the first time in days. "I wonder how the crops are doing?" he said aloud. Looking forward to getting his hands in the dirt, he flipped the reins and clicked as Smokey picked up the pace.

Both Ten and Smokey felt the tension of the wagon as it rattled and banged along the way, interrupting the peace of the ride home. He hadn't noticed the noise of the wagon as they took Simeon to Rockford. Was it Simeon's weight in the wagon helping the wheels roll gently over the holes in the road? Was it the task they had to complete? Was it the strange man's confusing message that made the wagon's creaks and bumps more irritating now? Ten didn't know, but he imagined he felt every bump as they worked their way home.

Ten and Smokey ambled down the hill and past the timber Ten had trimmed nine months ago. They headed towards the Fierce place. "The new fields are looking good." he thought as his gaze ran across the crops beginning to show life where he had planted them a short while ago. "We are going to have a good harvest!" he smiled to himself. Soon, he was pulling into the farmyard. Smoke was rising from Wils' shop, and Ten could hear him working away with the hot iron. Lottie was out back hanging laundry, the children running around her, hiding in her skirts, laughing, and playing tag. Chickens added to the commotion. Ten smiled as he thought of the love and warmth surrounding this family. "Do ya think? One day, maybe I can have a place and a family of my own too?" he dared to ponder the idea.

Still on the wagon, he stood up and hollered at Lottie. "Hey, Lottie!" he waved as she turned around and smiled. She came running with all the children trailing along behind, "Ten! Ten! Ten is here!" Everyone shouted and laughed. The children ran ahead of Lottie and started jumping and reaching up to give him a warm hug. Ten laughed and relished the love of family. He didn't feel so very alone now.

He jumped off the wagon, unhitched Smokey, releasing him to graze. Smokey shook his head, pawed the ground, and walked over to the water tank for a long drink. After Lottie and each of the children got a greeting, Ten stood up and looked at Lottie, "Is Wils in his shop?"

"Yes, he is, go on back there," she replied, "He'll be glad to see you."

Ten walked over to Wils blacksmith shop and stepped in. The door was wide open for fresh air, but Ten still felt a wall of heat as he entered. "Hey, Wils!" Shiny with sweat, Wils looked up and grinned. He looked back and put his irons down to cool.

"I'll just do that piece over," he said as he looked back up at Ten, "I just started anyway. How are you,

Ten!" The two men shook hands and patted each other on the back. The two had a genuine affection that ran deep. "How was your Pa?" Wils asked.

Ten's smile faded, "He's not good, but you know that. I don't know how long he will live. He's dying, and he knows it."

"Is that hospital a good place?"

"Yes, they will be able to take better care of him than Jane could have." Ten responded, adding, "You are right, Wils, she ain't a bad person. It's just more than she can handle. And Pa knows it. That's what matters. That he's okay with it all."

Wils nodded. "Well, I'm glad you got to take him."

"Wils, both Pa and I, we're grateful to you. I owe you everything."

"Aw Ten, this is about family. You do this for family. We can't survive unless we help each other. You are helping us now." Wils smiled warmly. "I know you still have a lot to work out, and you can do that right here with us."

Ten wondered what Wils meant by that. "Does he hear me at night?" Ten thought. "No," he stopped himself, "Don't start getting all suspicious, Ten. You could go crazy then. You've got enough to figure out without adding that to your list!"

Chapter 5

Endings

The rest of that year was canning vegetables, putting up hay, and hoeing. Because of Wils, they had a reaper, so cutting the wheat had been much more manageable. Ten and Duke took turns guiding the horse and reaper through the fields while the girls followed behind, tying small handfuls of sheaves together with straw. Ten or Wils would follow and pile the sheaves into stooks to dry in the field. The two went on to the next project while the girls kept watch over the wheat heads. Once thoroughly dry, they brought it in for processing and storage.

Now as Ten inspected the corn, the tassels had turned brown, and Ten could see the kernels were ready. It was time for harvest. Every year it seemed everything came ready at once. The days were long, and the whole family worked from dawn 'til dusk every day through the end of October. Even Wils came out for a few days. At night Ten fell into bed exhausted and hoping to no avail, Michael wouldn't appear.

Despite his night visitor, this was Ten's favorite time of year. He had forgotten the hitchhiker and his strange message. It was exciting to see the produce develop to harvest. Lottie and the girls handled all the processing, canning, drying, and storage. Ten would haul grain and produce for sale at the general store. As soon as the crops were in, Ten turned to clearing timber and preparing fields for the next season. This included cutting and splitting firewood for winter. Another year, the same thing over again. Ten loved the predictable tedium and solitary time out in the fields. Crowds were never his interest. He loved the cool shade on a hot summer day, and the sun's warmth on a cold winter day. It was all a joy to him until Michael popped up and interrupted him.

After Easter, 1866, Ten decided to head up for Rockford to see his pa. Without a wagon, he expected to make better time. He planned to head out early in the morning and get to either Sterling or Dixon for the night. Not wanting to get caught in a storm, Ten would judge from there whether he could get on up to Rockford by nightfall the next day. Lottie supplied him with jerky, biscuits, and beans for the trip. It felt good to be in the saddle again with

Smokey. As they rode off, Ten spoke out loud, "Just you and me this time, Smokey." It seemed Smokey felt the same, glad to be on the road, just the two of them and no wagons to haul. He nodded his head and whinnied.

The trip was cold but uneventful. Michael made his usual nightly visits. Ten had time to think about Michael's visits during the ride, and he realized his nightmares were now a routine part of his life. He just expected them. The shocking images were still horrific. He wondered if the adrenalin from the shock each night gave him the energy to stay on top of his work as morning rolled around. Alarmed that he needed Michael, Ten recalled the strange hitchhiker. "That guy, was he real or just another dream?" Ten wondered. "I understand this night visitor is just a nightmare memory. Maybe I should un-name him; I don't know why I gave him that honor in the first place." Ten said out loud, "Michael, forget it, you no longer have a name. You're only a bad memory." He spoke, firmly and it felt good to create distance from this nightly vision.

Ten arrived in Rockford late at night. He rode by the hospital and saw nothing had changed. It was late, so he decided to stay in a nearby boarding house choosing to come back in the morning. He'd never stayed in a boarding house, to him travel always meant camping along the trail. He had no idea what to expect. The boarding house was a large home renovated for this new purpose. The family lived on the first floor. One could see a small dining area to the left and a kitchen beyond the dining area upon entering the house. There was a desk at the base of the stairs in the foyer. Private family quarters were to the right, with a set of double doors protecting their privacy.

As he paid for his room, the woman provided her list of services, "You are late for dinner, but you can help yourself to what's left; it's back in the kitchen. My daughter is back there cleaning up And I will prepare a hot bath if you would like." She nodded to a door behind the staircase labeled 'bathing room.' Ten noticed it was the back porch boarded in.

Ten was overwhelmed. "Sure," he said.

Confused, the woman responded, "Does that mean you would like both? Some food and a bath?"

Ten smiled and said, "Yes, that would be fine."

She nodded toward the kitchen, "While I draw your bath, you go on back and grab some food, Katherine will help you. You eat in the dining area there. Here is the key to your room. It's upstairs and to your right."

Ten smiled and put the key in his pocket, turned, and headed back toward the kitchen, "Wow, this is nice. Wonder what the food is like?" The young lady back in the kitchen smiled as he walked in, pulled out what was left of dinner for him, and handed him a lovely blue floral dinner plate. "Thank you, ma'am." He said as he took the delicate plate awkwardly. He felt clumsy and held on tightly, worried he would drop it. She loaded it with beef, potatoes, a biscuit and finally poured a huge ladle of gravy over the whole plate of food. He walked carefully out of the kitchen, making sure not to spill, and sat down in the designated dining area. He sat straight and tall, not sure how to eat in such a fine room, and on such fine china. But after the first bite, he bent over the plate and ate ravenously. He'd never eaten such a great meal. As soon as it was gone, the young lady showed up, smiled, and took his plate.

"Would you like pie?" she asked.

Ten smiled in return and said, "No thanks." He was exhausted and dusty. He held back a burp until she had gone and tried to keep it quiet with his hands. After this incredible experience, he was looking forward to that warm bath. The tub was ready for him, and a folded towel lay on the chair beside the tub. A bar of soap and a scrub brush was placed on the table beside the tub. He relished the warmth slowly sinking into the warm water. "Is this what rich city life is like? And they are going to feed me breakfast, too!" He closed his eyes and soaked until he felt himself drifting into slumber.

It was one of those twilight moments that Ten rarely experienced anymore. He sensed a quiet darkness close in on him. He often felt this before his visitor's bright light would explode, interrupting his sleep. The hint of his night visitor startled him back to consciousness, successfully preventing the horrid vision from melting into his thoughts. "Best I don't fall asleep here." He said, "Besides, the water is getting cold."

Ten got out, dressed, and went up to his room. The bed was large, and there were piles of quilts spread out over the mattress. As he sat on the edge of the bed, he sank a good six inches. He looked at the mattress and stood up again, wondering if it was broken. Lifting up its side, he inspected the frame underneath supporting the soft plush mattress. Puzzled, he set it down. The mattress looked fine as he walked around testing each corner. It sank consistently wherever he sat. Shrugging his shoulders, he sat down one last time and took off his shoes before falling back onto the bed. Sleep came quickly.

Sure enough, his nightmare found him in that luxurious boarding house. Ten woke up with a yelp. He sat up surrounded by quilts and the soft mattress. Disoriented, he looked around while trying to figure out where he was. As the horrific image faded, he realized where he was. "Wow!" he thought. "This bed is way too soft." He tossed and turned for about an hour and then finally got up, grabbed a pillow, one thin quilt, and lay on the floor. "That's better," he thought and fell back to sleep.

The next morning, he came down to return his key and to eat breakfast. "Thank you, Mr. Gibbs. How did you sleep?" Ten looked at her gaze. Constantly wary that people would hear his night screams, he was sure she had heard.

"It was fine." Anxious to get away, he turned to the dining room for breakfast. Ham and eggs fried in grease, gravy, and potatoes, another wonderful hot meal. As he finished, he headed out the front door and around to the back of the house where they had boarded Smokey for the night. "How are you Smokey," he asked, glad to see his familiar old friend. All this new-fangled stuff was too much, and although the food was good, he was happy to be leaving. "Shall we get outta here?" Smokey was always ready for a ride with his man.

The Veteran's Hospital was just a half-mile from the boarding house, and they were there in just a few minutes. At the front, Ten slipped off his horse, throwing the reins over the post. He held his hat in hand, stepped up to the front door, and knocked. After a short wait, Marietta answered the door. "Hello ma'am, I brought my pa here last summer, and I just came to see him. Name was Simeon Gibbs?"

"Oh yes, I remember you. You fixed up a nice little tent for him on your wagon."

"That's right." he answered.

She didn't offer to let him in. Standing in the doorway, she looked at him silently for a moment, considering what to say. "I'm sorry, sir," She said slowly, "Your Pa isn't with us any longer. He died a while ago. We sent Jane a telegram. You need to talk to her. I'm sorry if she didn't tell you."

Ten's shoulders dropped in surprise. He quickly grabbed his hat as it slipped out of his fingers. "What?" he responded.

"I'm sure sorry. That's about all I can tell you."

"Thank you, ma'am." She watched sadly, as he turned away, walked back to Smokey, and hopped onto the saddle. Leaning slowly to the right, he guided Smokey away from the hospital. Marietta quietly closed the door. Ten nudged Smokey back the way they came. "I knew this was comin'." he thought. "I just liked to think of him here with Marietta watching over him." They rode slowly and quietly out of town toward Rock River and the path home. By the time he had gotten to Sterling, he had decided to go through Persifer and talk to Jane.

After a night in Sterling, he headed to Persifer and rode straight up to Jane's house. It was supper time, and she was feeding the children. He knocked loudly on the door. Ten heard much commotion of chairs being pushed around on the floor and children talking. Jane pulled open the door with an angry look on her face, children peering behind her. "Oh," she said as she recognized Ten. "I wondered, who was here this time of day"

"What happened to Pa?" he asked with no greeting.

"Ten," she realized why he was there, and her eyes shifted from anger to surprise. "He died. They sent me a telegram. Didn't say much. It just said: "*Your*

*husband died this afternoon. Shall we bury here?
Answer?"*

She waited a moment for a response. Ten said nothing. She went on, "So, I sent a telegram back that said 'yes.'"

"And you couldn't send one to me?" Surprised at how steely his voice sounded, Ten looked at her with dark eyes.

"No, Ten, didn't think of it." Jane looked sincerely sorry. "There is so much going on, and I have very little money to do that."

Ten was angry and continued to stand there motionless on her doorstep, suddenly feeling the chill of a cool March evening. "Where is he buried?"

"I don't know, Ten." she said, and then she added hesitantly, "They didn't tell me that." Then with a bit of a whimper, "I'm just surviving here, Ten."

"But you could have told me." He turned to leave.

As he walked to Smokey, Jane spoke again, "Ten, you need to know." Ten stopped but didn't turn around, "I just got engaged. I'm going to marry again come February. I won't be here much longer."

Ten said nothing and walked on back to Smokey. Jane watched him ride away.

It would be a cold night, and Ten didn't know what to do or where to go right then. "We'll ride awhile, I guess, and then camp along the river. Smokey, we been along here plenty now, and I know a good spot." They resumed their journey home and headed down the road. "I told myself I wouldn't come back and here I am. It was a waste of time." Ten dreaded telling Wils and Lottie the news.

Holly Bohling

Chapter 6

Healing

Ten got back to the Fierce farm late the next night, quietly taking care of Smokey and putting him out to pasture for a good night's rest. Ten watched Smokey ambling toward the oak tree on the hill, turned to the bunkhouse, and slipped into his bed. As usual, he was up early the following morning, this time of year, before the birds began chirping. First were chores, and as he started moving about the yard, he was impressed that Duke had done an excellent job the few days he was gone. As the household began to stir, Ten began thinking through what he would tell the family. Waving at Ten as if he'd never been gone, the children came streaming out to tend to their chores. Today they were feeding the dogs spare meat scraps. It triggered much barking among the dogs. Sometimes, if the boys had gone hunting the day before these scraps included rabbits and birds. It was important to keep the two dogs (Stet and Chet) healthy as they were to guard the chickens and other livestock from hawks, coyotes, and whatever else tried to come along for a chicken dinner. They needed healthy dogs with full stomachs feel no need to eat the small livestock. The children checked daily for newly laid eggs, and every day they ran back and forth to the well with pails to fill the water tank.

When Lottie had breakfast ready, she called the family back in to eat. Everyone wrapped up what they were doing and headed to the house. Ten lagged a bit, trying to think how he would break the news about Pa. Lottie waited for him at the door, "Hey Ten, good to see you back." Lottie knew by his face the news was not good. "Umm, that was a quick trip." She didn't want his update on Pa yet, so she went on, "Hurry up, we're ready to eat."

He stepped in and sat down in his usual spot, not feeling very hungry. He took a strip of pork and a biscuit. Everyone was talking, sharing stories about what they had seen during their morning chores. How many eggs were laid that day, whether any coyote tracks or scat were lying, around and who stole the covers last night? The boys said the dogs, Stet and Chet, were especially hungry this morning and wondered how busy their night had been.

Eventually, the children got up and headed back outside. Lottie delayed getting up, knowing it was best to wait 'til the children left to ask how the trip to

Rockford had gone. "Okay, Ten, let's hear it, what happened?"

He looked at her, and all his planning disappeared, "He's dead, Lottie."

"What?" she responded. "Why didn't we know?"

"They sent a telegram to Jane asking her if they should bury him. She told them to go ahead. She has no idea where he is buried!"

"What?" She said again. Wils sat and chewed his last bite of food, not knowing what to say.

"The nurse couldn't tell me what happened, so I went to see Jane in Persifer. She had some excuse why she didn't send us a telegram, too busy, too poor. I don't know." Words came flying out of his mouth.

"When did it happen?"

"Uhm," Ten responded, "I didn't ask. I was so upset."

"So, he's gone, and we didn't have a chance to say good-bye." Lottie began to cry. "Both of them are gone now. There is no ma or pa anymore." She realized how selfish that sounded and looked at Ten, "You know what I mean? We're in the same boat."

"But Lottie," Wils spoke up, "We have each other. Ten is here; we have all our children. Our lives are full. Your Pa was tired and ready to be with the Lord in heaven."

"There's more," Ten said. "Jane is getting married in February."

Wils continued to take the lead, "You both know that sometimes that happens. Marriage is a good thing. We need a life partner. Her time with your Pa was short, and we all know it was almost a business arrangement for them. She was loyal 'til he died."

Lottie and Ten ignored his comments. Both knew that people remarried all the time. Maybe it was because they'd just heard about Pa, but it just seemed too soon. Ten wondered to himself, "I am 22; maybe I should be thinking about a wife." He abruptly stopped and shook his head, thinking, "No, I'm not ready. Besides, people keep dying on me. I'll stay single and work here at the Fierce farm. That's my plan." Lottie was crying. Ten stood up, "I'd better get back out there. I'll take Duke with me; we need to get the crops in, time's a-wastin'."

Days went by as Ten and Duke got the crops planted. In the evenings, Ten would hunt for logs to build a one-room house for Phietta. His goal was to have Smokey drag one log in each evening. Lottie asked him to take a break, but he refused. He agreed to go to church on Sundays, but he would ride Smokey, so he could leave right after services and get back to work. He became quite celebrated around the house for his words, "Time's a-wastin'."

One evening Wils rode out to join Ten, saying he just needed a break from smithin'. Ten knew there was a conversation coming. While they were hunting for the perfect tree, Wils mentioned Phietta. "You know Ten; she wants to see if Sam comes back."

"He's not gonna." Ten responded. "When that lust for gold gets in your blood, it's hard to shake. I had friends in the war that were headed to Wyoming and Idaho when they got out. They couldn't quit talking about fortunes out west. They call it 'gold fever.' She needs to come live with us here."

"I know Ten; I'm just not sure when that will be."

"Well, this house will be ready when she comes. I plan on getting it up by early September before the harvest has to come in."

"I knew you would say something like that, so I sent her a letter letting her know you were working on a place for her and that it will be waiting until she's ready. I haven't heard back yet."

The two men began chopping away, alternating, and enjoying the cool evening breeze.

Wils said, "It just needs to be one room. We will share the main house for kitchen and washing." In August 1866, Phietta sent them a letter explaining that she still wanted to wait for Sam. He had been sending money, and she hoped he would come for her and the children. Wils read the letter to Lottie and Ten.

"Shall we keep working on her place?" Wils asked Ten.

"Of course, we will build it. Phietta may not be coming now, but she will eventually. I can bring in the harvest, and we'll work on the house after that." Thankful for long summer days, Ten, Wils, and Duke were able to bring in all the logs needed for a small one-room house to accommodate Phietta and her four children. They found a level spot close to the bunkhouse and spent the next couple of winters building the house during their downtime. Duke was getting quite proficient in the fields and good at fending off coyotes, cougar, and bears.

All through the fall of 1868 and winter 1869, they listened to the news about the presidential campaign. When anyone went into town, they came back with Les' updates from the general store. Les seemed to be most current with the national news. Ten even began staying longer after church to hear what else locals might know. Ten was 23 years old now, and it was his first year to vote for president. During the social gatherings after church, he was proud to declare he would vote for Ulysses S Grant. "I served under him in the army; he can be my president now." Ten told the rest.

Wils agreed and also planned on voting for Grant. In addition, he announced he was joining the Prohibition Party. The newly formed group was dedicated to ending the consumption of alcohol. "Lottie," Wils explained, "We watched Jasper down the hill kill himself with drink. It made him a different man. The toll it took on his family was devastating, and then he went and rolled the wagon on top of himself." Neither Lottie nor Ten responded. They knew Jasper's story. "Right now, the party is just saying moderate your drinking, but I am one hundred percent for total prohibition!"

"How will we have communion then?" Lottie asked?

"I hear the Methodists have a special grape juice that works," Wils replied.

"I'm not so sure," Lottie replied. "I need to ask Pastor Henry what he thinks of that."

"Well, let me know what he says," Wils replied.

To the relief of the whole town, the election of Ulysses S. Grant as President was a landslide. Surprisingly the South voted for him too. No one knew how the South would vote; and after this election, Americans, thankfully, felt the division within the country was finally healing. Ulysses S. Grant was inaugurated as president of the United States on March 4, 1869.

By spring Phietta's new home was nearly ready, and the men tinkered at finish work through Summer 1869. Lottie was pregnant with Ira, and the baby was pulling too much energy from her. Lottie had a hard time keeping up with the daily routine of farm life. And was sick much of the time. Ten worried, remembering how his mother faded during her last pregnancy. By the fall of 1869, Margaret and Sarah had taken over the household duties, laundry, cleaning, cooking, and preparing harvest for storage and sale. Ira was born late in the year of 1869, and all Lottie could do was care for Ira. Margaret and Sarah continued with the household duties while Lottie rested between feeding Ira and herself.

Ten's successful farming was overwhelming the girls as they processed the harvest that fall of 1869, and Wils was worried they wouldn't be able to keep up without Lottie's help. The winter of 1870 was hard on the family as Lottie continued to fade. By early that summer Wils decided to write Phietta asking her to come live with them and help Phietta. Phietta wrote back, "Your letter came at a great time. Sam quit sending money, and I filed for divorce. I cannot afford to stay here any longer and have to leave. I am so happy for your offer and am deeply thankful to come help you and Lottie."

Wills was happy to hear the news and read the letter to Lottie and Ten. "Actually," Wils told them, "I can use a break from smithing. I'll get Phietta and bring her back. That way, you can get the harvest in."

Ten was relieved with that idea and nodded, "Sure thing. Duke, the kids and I can do harvest, and take care of things here. Lottie was thankful that Phietta would be around to help. In the meantime, Margaret and Sarah continued working the produce and watching the little children."

Wills wasted no time in bringing Phietta to her new home. It was ready and waiting for her by September of 1870. Phietta brought her four children, two boys, and two girls. William, the oldest at 21, an experienced farmer, was a great addition. Ten and William had some brief conversation about what William could take over when they got to the Fierce place.

Phietta and her family settled quickly in their new place. Ten had installed a wall inside to divide the space into three rooms. Phietta slept on one end of the main room. A worktable and chairs on the other end served as day space for the family. The children played and slept in the second room. William had the third room. Wils and Lottie suggested to Phietta that Ten might want the bunkhouse to himself for a while. Soon Phietta realized why. Her place was close to the bunkhouse, and she heard Ten's cry the first night. She was a much more straightforward person than either Lottie or Wils. Soon after her arrival, she followed him to the barn early one morning and asked, "Ten, I'm a light sleeper and, um, I hear you at night." She waited expectantly for a reply.

He kept busy spreading hay in the barn and shrugged. "Just nightmares from my time in the war." He didn't say anything more. Phietta waited a while and realized that's all she was going to hear, so she turned around and walked out of the barn. Ten paused and looked up at the barn wall and realized this meant Wils and Lottie had probably heard him as well. He believed this is why he should never marry, "Who would ever consider me?" He felt so very lonely, looking out the barn door as Phietta walked away into the morning light.

He didn't want to be alone. Ten realized that these night dreams stopped him from considering marriage. "What do you want from me? What do I have to do to make you go away?" He asked his visiting nightmare. The long-forgotten hitchhiker's words came to mind. His message was: "Let it go so you can move on with life." Fighting off the sense of loneliness, Ten paused before resuming his chores. He considered his life, the people he has loved, "I like solitude, always have, but solitude is not loneliness. Loneliness is different. It sucks you into nothingness." He began to reconsider, "Maybe I would like to marry." The thought surprised him.

Phietta was so very grateful for a place to live, she worked hard to be sure Lottie and Wils knew she would carry her weight. She took over all the cooking and processed the harvest with the help of the girls. She even helped tutor the children. Despite her help, Lottie continued to get worse. She was too weak to fight any longer and died July 1871, 18 months after their son Ira was born.

Michael, the Hitchhiker Returns

Ten had a hard time with Lottie's loss. His night visitor came multiple times a night. The lack of sleep made him short-tempered. Early one morning, Ten grabbed an ax and marched out to the timber. After walking for a good hour, he was sure no one could hear him; he cried out, "Why?" He took the ax and began swinging at a tree trunk. With each whack, he yelled out: "Why?" whack. "Do," whack. "They," whack. "Die?" whack. With each word, another Whack! Exhausted, he leaned against a neighboring tree. Looking at the cuts in the trunk, Ten realized he must finish chopping down the tree, so it wouldn't die and fall on its own. He slowly rose to his feet and stepped forward to finish the final cuts. He stopped as he felt the tree shift and heard it crackle. Looking up the massive trunk, his eyes gazed through the leaves, and he focused on the deep blue sky above. "So beautiful!" he thought as he gently pushed the tree to assist the fall. The tree landed with a loud thump, and the ground rumbled beneath Ten's feet. Feeling a sense of peace, Ten picked up the ax he had dropped and gazed at the sky. Turning back toward the house, he stopped abruptly. There in front of him stood Michael, the hitchhiker.

"Hi, Ten," Michael smiled at Ten's surprise.

"Well, I didn't think I'd ever see you again." Ten commented. "Actually, I began to think you were just my imagination."

"Interesting, so is your other visitor. I'm glad you stopped calling him Michael. I was taking that personally!" Michael smiled at his weak joke. "Remember, those visions are just images buried in your memory bank."

Ten sat down on the brand-new tree stump anticipating more.

Michael sat on the fallen log across from Ten. "I've been watching. You are doing well. Wils needs you now, but he will soon be fine. Phietta is here to help. And her son, William, will be staying on to help with farm work. You have trained them all well.

"Ten, the spring of your life is over. I am here to tell you, send your visitor away. Be firm, be strong, and it will go away. The future is yours to claim. You must dare to dream for the future. Dare to hope. Only you can do that, but you _can_ do it."

"I don't understand, it's like a memory haunting me. It's the same every time."

"As I said before, it's a memory frozen in your mind from a time long past. You won't eliminate the memory, and you will always be sad about it. But so far, you have *allowed* that memory to move forward in time with you and haunt you night after night. Now *you must* send it away...with conviction. Take this moment, enjoy today, live in the moment, and allow yourself to dream for the future. That nightmare will stop. And, Ten, you started today!"

Ten frowned, "How?"

"While you chopped down this tree, you told it to go away. Don't you feel more peace now than you've had in a long time?"

Ten realized the hitchhiker was right. He felt a calming peace inside of him.

Michael went on, "It may come back once in a while. Such dreams don't seem to stop all at once. Just keep sending it away. When you have that dream, spread your arms out wide and demand it to go away. With force! You can say anything. It might be nice to add a little something like, "In God's name, I've had enough! Go away." But be firm about it."

"Okay," Ten said meekly.

Michael frowned, "Well, that was a bit weak, but you will get the hang of it. Like I said, what you did just a minute ago was a good first step.

"Another thing, Ten, here is something you might dream about. I've seen a fine young lady at your church; her name is Sarah Jane. She is spicy, and she will be a fine woman and a good wife. She would be a good one for you to consider."

Ten cocked his head as he tried to figure this guy out. "Okay..." he said again.

"I've stayed as long as I can. Good to talk to you." Michael turned and walked back into the timbers. This time Ten didn't follow.

Holly Bohling

Chapter 7

New Beginnings

In October 1871, just months after Lottie's death, Wils joined Ten in the field. Ten always knew that meant a serious conversation was going to happen. It was a pattern for Wils. It was easy for the two of them to talk out there without interruption. Ten waited for Wils to catch up, and they began walking through the field. "Ten, I know it hasn't been long, but I need to tell you, Phietta and I have decided to marry," he paused, "in March."

Ten stopped walking. He was surprised, as he thought to himself, "It's Phietta, my sister." He wished happiness for her, but this was a surprise. By now, Ten knew that's what people do; and he knew Wils was deeply dedicated to Ten's family. Ten remembered his Pa married Jane so quickly, and then Jane married again soon after Pa died. Ten was trying to absorb it all. "I suppose people just can't afford to take the time to grieve!"

"Yes," Wils said. "Ten, I love your whole family. We go way back. And I love Phietta. I will always love Lottie, and I can love Phietta too."

"I understand Wils, and I know she will be happy with you. You are a good man, and Phietta deserves a good man. I know you have love in your heart for her. It's just, it's just," Ten thought about what to say, "so soon. Lottie has been gone only a couple of months. I'm still missing her."

"I know Ten, but I am a man, and I see her in my house every day. With the love and affection, I have for her, we need to marry."

Ten understood what Wils meant by that. "I understand. If you are asking me, you have my blessing."

Wils was relieved to hear this. The wedding plans began as the holidays approached. Then, soon after the holidays, Ten had another surprise. While the family sat at dinner, Duke announced his plans to marry Elizabeth. Ten knew Elizabeth was a neighbor who lived a couple of miles down the road. Duke had an eye on her for years. Ten just hadn't noticed they had started courting. "Incredulous!" Ten thought, then he said aloud, "My work must be blinding me. I just don't see these things going on."

Duke laughed. Clearly, Wils and Phietta already knew as they smiled at Ten. Smiling in return, Ten looked down at his plate.

"We will marry in June, so Pa and Phietta can have their wedding before us."

Ten nodded his head. "Congratulations Duke, Elizabeth is a good choice. I am happy for you." Ten had learned by now never to expect things to stay constant. He rolled his eyes and smiled at Duke. "And what's next?" he exclaimed with a big smile.

"Actually," Duke responded, "We plan to homestead out west. We've heard Kansas is a great place." Duke went on, "Her folks are going too. With William here to help Pa on the farm, I can move on. We will be leaving soon after the wedding!"

Wils smiled weakly. He knew this was coming and still needed to prepare for the idea that his oldest son would be leaving. Ten thought, "Sure enough, Michael was right, we must move on. Things keep changing. I must take hold of my own future." He watched Wils gaze at his son and felt the bittersweet happiness Wils felt for Duke.

Two weddings lined up against each other. First Wils and Phietta were married in March and two months later Duke and Elizabeth. The night before the March wedding, Wils pulled Ten aside, "There are a lot of weddings going on here. Have you thought much about it for yourself?"

Ten didn't like to talk about this but responded, "Yes, I have. I've not been ready before. But maybe it's time."

Wils went on, "A woman would be right proud to have you as a husband. You have established yourself, saved up money to start out on your own, and there's your pension. That's what parents of a young lady want for their daughter."

Ten hadn't thought of it that way. He'd never thought about courtship and what it might require. It made him shiver inside. Wils explained, "Ten, you have what it takes to be a good family man, and you should make plans for that. If nothing else, Ten, just take a look at the women out there. The church is a good place to find a good woman. Besides Ten, think about it; there aren't many good men out there. So many died in the war."

Ten looked at Wils on that comment remembering what Michael said to him, "There is a fine young woman at your church, called Sarah Jane."

After the weddings were over, Duke left for Kansas. He wrote often and described his new place and seemed excited about his new beginnings. He would not be a blacksmith, but he had learned some ironwork and saved money on blacksmith fees and repairs. Wils read the letters at dinner time, sharing Duke's story with the family. Hearing of Duke's adventures gave Ten a twinge of excitement for a similar experience.

Now that Wils and Phietta were married and Duke was gone, Ten focused on making sure William was ready to take over his work. Ten considered moving west too. And then, over the summer Ten even began to think about marriage, "Maybe it is time." But although his nightmares were not as intense, they still happened regularly. He worried about his worthiness for marriage until these night dreams were gone.

Harvest season picked up in September 1872, and an intense thunderstorm blew in and was wreaking havoc in the night. With a tremendously loud thunderclap, his slumber suddenly flipped into his nightmare. Moments later, lightning crashed, with another burst of thunder following the flash; and the familiar blood red eyes burst into view. Ten screamed, jumped out of bed, and ran out the door and into the night. As the rain poured on him, he kept running, yelling, "Noooo!" Each burst of lighting startled him, and he screamed. Flash! He ducked and tucked into a bush, grabbing for his rifle. But there was no rifle. He felt helpless with no weapon. Thunder roared, and he cringed under the bush. Flash! He darted right and left as if avoiding gunfire. Flash! He collapsed in the rain and darkness. With his eyes closed, he stretched out, face up, on the ground and let the rain pour over his face. "Oh, Lord, please, just one night!" He begged for a night's sleep without this nightmare. "Forgive me and take him away!" Ten stopped short and rose to his knees, back straight and strong. He stretched out his arms. "Forever! Make him go away! Forever!" As he looked into the sky, rain continued to wash over his face. Blinking through raindrops he cried out, "In God's name, take this away!"

He collapsed to the ground in a fetal position, exhausted. The heavy rain slowed. He started to take deep, slow breaths, smelling the wet forest air. Peace came over him as he was reminded of his love for this countryside. After a moment he lifted his head, "It's over." Not knowing why those words came to mind, he sat up to look around. The wind was calm, and the lightning was a mere silent twinkle in the distance. As the thunder faded, the storm within him subsided.

Ten slowly got to his feet and stood sopping wet from the hard rain. Reaching out his arms, he looked to the night sky and the dark swirling clouds. He spoke to his hitchhiker. "Michael, was that you? Did you blow the storm away?" Ten paused and then added confidently, "Michael, I did it! As you said, I sent him away." He took a long deep cleansing breath and exhaled slowly. "It feels good. I know, it's gone." He saw stars begin to peek out from behind the clouds as they drifted apart. "Now, I will wait to see if it lasts." Ten stood in silence as if to wait for an answer. Nothing but silence surrounded him as the storm to fades in the distance. Finally, Ten sat down on a tree stump he'd cut earlier.

He spoke to his hitchhiker friend, "You know Michael, time keeps ticking no matter where I am. Every day the sun comes up. At night the moon comes round. Winter is cold, and the snow falls. Summer sizzles. Every year I plant; I chop; feed livestock, and birth calves. When I feel the weather change, I know what needs to be done. Time carries me through each new day. Every year, it's the same, I know what I must do and when. And yet, it's different every year. But I really didn't know what I needed to do... until now. Your message makes sense now. Thank you, Michael."

He looked around. He realized he'd come to the field he'd cleared that first fall after his return from the war. He saw the first shoots of wheat settling down as the storm winds subsided. He remembered the beauty of their rich golden shafts flowing in the breeze. He spoke as if someone were sitting next to him, "When these shafts of wheat glow golden, they reign over the fields in all their fullness and glory! And then, they die." He paused, "These shafts seem to know what's coming. They pour all their energy to fulfill their purpose in life, leaving behind tiny seeds carrying the promise of a new life in a new time." Ten was thankful, "The work I do is good; it brings joy even when I am sad."

He gazed across the countryside, "I finally see the rhythm of life in all of this. With every tree I plant, one dies. The potatoes bring fruit for the next season. The dog grows old, but a new puppy is born. Ma and Pa are gone. Lottie is gone." He took a deep breath. "All good things have their moment. But we all must move on, and so shall I. We must make room for the new. Today is good!"

Slapping his hands on his knees, Ten stood up, "I am ready. I will remember these moments and the precious people that have been in my life." Ten smiled and watched the stars, "But, right now, this is my time now. I claim it. I will live fully and richly through my golden days, like the wheat thrives for a golden moment before harvest. In the end, leaving fruit for future generations." Ten paused and imagined the shaft of next summer waving in the breeze. He looked up toward Wils' homestead.

Suddenly he realized how cold he'd become. He shivered and decided to run back to his room. It was a quiet run, peaceful and calm, as cleansing breeze brushed against him, and the cool air brought the sweet scent of damp trees. Ten felt as if his hitchhiker friend, Michael, was telling him, "Good job Ten, go and live."

The days were different for Ten now. He woke up with the same passion for working the fields, but it was for the love and beauty of the work. No longer was he running away from his nightmare. Phietta and Wils noticed something had changed but could not figure out why he seemed so content. Then one morning as they woke, Wils looked at Phietta and said, "You know, I haven't heard him cry out in the night. I wonder if that is over?"

Phietta looked at him and whispered back, "You know, you are right! Oh my, that's why he looks content!" Wils had always encouraged Ten to join them for church, but Ten always felt unworthy. However, even though it was harvest season, Ten had a renewed interest in church and allowed Wils to make him go. He didn't know many people other than the other farmers. Now he began looking around the congregation wondering who that girl was that Michael mentioned. Looking around, Ten asked himself, "What was that name? Sarah something?"

Ten had noticed a busy young girl at Wils and Phietta's wedding last spring. He saw her again at Duke's wedding. She had been busy with the children, surrounding her as they laughed and played. Now, he went to church, and he looked for her. He even stayed after services for the social hour. He spotted her. "Hey, Wils, who is that girl over there?" Ten tipped his head to the side, trying to be discreet. Wils was not helpful at all as he turned visibly towards the young girl. "Oh her," he said out loud, "That's Sarah Rogers, spunky thing, she is." Wils turned back to Ten and suddenly realized what was on Ten's mind. A smile came across Wils' face. "Ahhh, Ten," Wils said, "She would be a good choice. She is smart, the children love her, and she is strong. She even works hard helping her pa in the fields. She'd be a good wife for a farmer like you."

Wils was eager to tell him more. "You know her pa, Jacob. A good man and a good friend."

Embarrassed, Ten looked the other direction and nodded; he knew Jacob. "Sarah," he thought. "Is that the name Michael gave me?" He looked at Wils, "I need to think about it."

Ten wasn't interested in pursuing much until the harvest was over, and then the brutal winter months came. Often, they couldn't even navigate the snow to get to church. Ten spent the early months of spring preparing for planting season. He didn't have much time to think about girls. "Ten," Wils approached Ten, "I know you are nervous about courting someone. I can tell because you keep finding excuses to delay. You need to take the leap!"

One Sunday in May, he noticed Sarah again during a Sunday church picnic. Ten and Wils chatted with Jacob, her father. Ten noticed, Harriett, Sarah's mother, stayed close to Jacob, allowing Sarah to manage all the little ones during the picnic. Ten liked getting to know her parents. It would make things easier when the time comes. Sarah joined in the games and fun with her friends while skillfully watching her little siblings. Ten frowned as he saw one of the young boys, about 15 showing interest in Sarah. He ran up to her and threw pulled grass on her hair. Sarah seemed to blush, laughed, turned, and ran after him. Quickly she remembered her siblings and went back to her duties. As the picnic ended, she had the little ones help gather the mess to help clean up. "Sarah is quite the worker." thought Ten. "She clearly loves to be with people and still gets things done. And she's pretty!" At that moment, Ten decided then it was time, "I'm going to do it. I know her folks. I can do this."

That night Ten's old nightmare began to stir in Ten's mind, but Ten woke before it was able to create its horror. Ten sat up and said calmly but firmly, "Stop this!" It faded instantly. Ten smiled and realized he was winning this battle. He directed his thoughts to something more exciting. He thought of Sarah and what he might say to her parents about possible courtship. With these new thoughts and the hope of a new future, Ten smiled, lay down, and fell asleep.

The following morning, he joined Wils in his shop. "Wils, I'm going to ask Mr. and Mrs. Rogers for permission to court Sarah." Wils looked at Ten and broke into a huge grin.

"That's a mighty fine idea." Wils slapped Ten on the back. "She is a handful, but you are perfect for her. Nothing frazzles you and she can work as hard as you. You will make a good team."

Ten smiled when Wils said, 'nothing frazzles you.' "You have no idea," thought Ten. Then aloud, he said, "Maybe that's true now, but there was a day..."

Wils went on, "I'm happy for you. Whatever you want to do. You can stay here with us, or you can get a place for a new life with your own family. We can move William to the bunkhouse, and you can have that place we built for Phietta when she first moved here." Wils paused and realized he was moving too quickly. Getting back to courtship, he went on, "Let's talk more tonight. Phietta and I can give you some tips when you ask her folks about courtship. I've been around that bush a couple of times." He winked and smiled.

Ten smiled, not sure he was interested in advice, "Thanks, Wils, I have money, never needed to use it, so I've saved enough. But now that you mention it, maybe it would be good to have our own place."

Ten was not willing to wait any longer. His courage was up, and Ten did not want to delay in case the courage failed him. So the next Sunday, he found Jacob Rogers standing outside visiting with some of the other elders. Ten approached him and said, "May I have a word with you, sir?"

Jacob looked at Ten and said, "Of course, Ten." As they stepped aside, Jacob asked, "Just wondering, I didn't know you then, but aren't you that young man that helped Ol' Gus with the crazy guy?"

Ten looked embarrassed, "Yes, that was quite a while ago, sir."

"Why yes, it was. But I just thought of asking you now. Anyway, what do you want, Ten?"

"Can we step over here?" as Ten moved towards Smokey, tied to the post at the Church's front entry. Privately Ten thought this would allow for a quick escape if Jacob did not respond well.

Jacob nodded and followed Ten. "Can I stop by your house this afternoon? I have a question for you and Mrs, Rogers."

"Well, Ten, we will get home about 4 PM. Can you tell me what it's about?"

"I'd like to wait 'til Mrs. Rogers is present." Ten was trying to sound casual and formal at the same time and failing miserably.

"Sure, we will be home." Jacob nodded.

Ten put his hand to the brim of his hat and tipped it slightly and smiled. "Thank you, sir. I'd best be off; much to do today." Relieved it was over, Ten jumped onto Smokey and trotted off.

That afternoon, Ten arrived at the Roger's home and found it was quiet. He walked up to the door, and with a deep sigh, knocked. Jacob answered quickly. "Hi, Ten, been expecting you. Come on in."

Mrs. Rogers was in her rocker near the stove, knitting. "Hi Ten," Harriett smiled at him. "Come sit here." Ten was thankful Mr. and Mrs Rogers made things comfortable for him. It was quiet in the house. And as Ten looked around wondering where everyone was, Mrs Rodgers added, "The children stayed back at church; Sarah is watching them. The Franklin's will bring them home shortly."

He was relieved to hear Sarah had stayed back at church with another family. Ten sat and rested his elbows on his knees with his hat in hand. "I guess y'all are wondering why I'm here."

"Well, Ten, we might have a good idea. But why don't you tell us." Jacob smiled and sat on the other side of Ten, not giving Ten a break from the awkward moment.

Ten tried to hide his shaking hands. "Well, I'm here because I've decided it's time for me to look for a wife. I have saved up some money to get started; I have a good pension from my service in the war." Ten paused and thought to himself, "I'm stalling." He took another breath and went on, "I've noticed your daughter Sarah and I see she is a fine young woman. I was hoping you would allow me to court her." Ten took a deep sigh as he finished.

Mr. Rogers broke into a big smile. "Well, Ten, we've noticed you since you came back from the war. You are a fine young man. So, when you asked to stop by, we thought you might be coming for something like this. The missus and I, we talked about it before you got here."

Mrs. Rogers interrupted. "Jacob told me that you are the young man who helped Ol' Gus. You are strong, proud, and courageous."

Mr. Rogers claimed the floor again, "And we would be right proud if you wanted to court her."

Ten looked at Mr. Rogers and then to Mrs. Rogers as they watched him fiddle with his hat thinking, "What have I gotten myself into?"

Sarah's parents went on, "You need to know Ten; she is a spunky young lady and has a mind of her own. It will take a strong man to handle her. We think you are that strong man." Unfortunately, Ten didn't pick up on that warning, but he would find out soon enough what they meant.

Ten stood up, still holding his hat, "Well, thank you, folks. I'll be calling on Sarah soon. Is next Friday evening, okay?" Jacob stood while Harriett continued knitting. "We will tell her tonight that you will be calling on her and that we approve." As Ten closed the door behind him, he looked up and saw Sarah hopping off the wagon, giggling as she gathered her younger siblings at the end of the driveway and waved good-by to those in the wagon. Ten thought, "Looks like she's had a good time." She turned toward the house and saw Ten mount his horse. He looked up as he sat down and noticed the boy that flirted with her sitting at the back of the wagon. Surprised by the emotion, a wave of jealousy filled him. "Well, I have her parent's ok. The first step is done!" He thought. She walked toward the house as Ten urged Smoky to start moving. He smiled and nodded at Sarah, tipping his hat. Sarah stared at him with a curious look and ran into the house with the children running behind.

As he rode away, he thought of Sarah. "She sure is cute. I hope she likes me." Another new feeling filled him, one of excitement and romance.

Chapter 8

Tomorrow's Dream

Sarah ran into the house, calling, "Hi Mother, Hi Father." It had been a wonderful afternoon, and she was excited that Billy seemed to like her. Harriett was still sitting in her rocker. Jacob was standing near the door.

"Hello, dear." Harriett said, "We have something to tell you. Come sit down."

Sarah did not like the sound of this. They never asked her to sit down at this time of day. It was time to prepare dinner. "What's going on?" she asked.

"Well, dear, you know that young man that just left?" Harriett went on.

"Yes, I saw him." Sarah had seen him at church but never paid much attention to adults.

"You are growing up, and we need to think about your future. It is time you consider becoming a wife and having a family."

Sarah frowned. She didn't like where this was going.

"That fine young man is interested in courting you," Jacob spoke up.

"What?" Sarah responded.

"That fine young man, Ten Gibbs, has asked us if he can court you and we have agreed." Jacob went on.

"What?" Sarah said again as she stood up.

"Ten would like to get to know you better and for you to get to know him." Harriett tried to soften the idea.

"NO!" Sarah yelled. "But, Billy likes me! I know it. He's cute. That man, Ten? He's old!" She turned and ran out the door. Harriett and Jacob looked at each other, bewildered.

After some silence, Harriett looked at Jacob and said, "I will talk to her tonight."

That evening, Harriett asked Sarah to sit down with her. Of course, Sarah knew this was to be a discussion about that 'Ten Gibbs.' Sure enough, Harriett opened with, "Sarah, you need to understand it is our decision whom you are to marry. It is not your decision."

Sarah silently looked at her feet. Her mother continued, "We know what is best for you. We have investigated Ten and what he brings to a marriage. Ten is a talented farmer; he is smart, he works hard, and on top of that, he's courageous. He gets a pension from his time serving in the war. Do you know what a pension is?"

"No," Sarah responded.

"He gets money every month from the government for the rest of his life. So you will get some even after he dies." Harriett explained. "It is recognition for his service to our country.'

Unimpressed and strong-minded, Sarah rebelled, "He's even shorter than some of the boys in school. You can't make me do anything!" She stormed out of the house and headed to the barn to get away from her mother. Once in the barn, she stopped and looked around, not sure what to do with herself. She knew her mother and father had decided.

Her mother quietly stepped into the barn behind Sarah. "Honey, I know this is hard for you. But think about it, haven't you noticed how many men went to fight and never came back? I can name a few; there's Gregory and Henry. There's more. You don't understand how lucky you are that a man like this is interested in you. So many women will never have an opportunity to marry or ever have a family."

Sarah calmed down. "Ma, I don't like being told what to do."

"You should be flattered. You are worthy of a good man. You certainly don't want to become an old maid." Her ma was hopeful they were getting somewhere. She paused as Sarah stood frowning with her arms crossed. Finally, Harriet decided to be firm. "Your pa has decided."

"It is not for Pa to say who I marry. It's for me to say. It's my life! He is old too old for me."

Harriett responded, "I understand, but it's not your choice."

"I do have a choice, and I choose NO!"

"There are girls your age that won't ever have anyone even show interest. We've lost so many good men. Sarah, letters never written. Letters never read." Harriet paused so Sarah could think about that, then went on, "Ten came home! There are women that will never have a suitor. You do!" Again, Harriett hesitated for emphasis, "Do you want to have children and your own place?"

"Yes," Sarah replied, but quickly added, "but not with him."

"You need a man that can take care of you. You are a perfect age to marry and bear children. He needs children to help on the farm, and that is your job." Finally, Harriet had enough, she stepped toward the door. "This is the last we will talk about it. He is going to court you, and you must give him the courtesy of spending time with him. We've raised you to be a proper young lady. He is a good man, and you may discover you might even like him!"

As she reached the door, an idea came to Harriett, "Did you also know he is the man who helped Ol' Gus in the stable some months ago, from that crazy guy?"

"No, I didn't." Sarah responded. "But I still don't want to marry him."

Harriett was silent, looking at her daughter, waiting. Sarah looked at her mother and after a long silence, and sighed, "Okay Ma, I'll give him a chance." And a little more loudly, "But I don't like it."

"Okay then. It's settled." Harriett turned and walked back to the house leaving Sarah standing in the barn. Sarah had just turned 15.

It was early December as Ten planned for their first meeting. After a good bath, haircut, and shave, he combed his mustache and made sure the ends curled up nicely. Phietta advised Ten to take something pretty for his first visit, suggesting some pussy willow branches she had dried. Finding additions to the bouquet would be difficult as the snow was lying on the ground, and there were no flowers to gather from the garden. Thinking of Lottie and her love for her garden, he went out and gathered some dried milo berry stems, dried ornamental grass, and greens from the pine trees and pinecones. They came together to make a pretty holiday collection. As he put the bouquet together, he thanked Lottie for bringing beauty to the farm. He took some time to grieve for her. It seemed like yesterday, but so long ago. He marveled at how time plays games with your mind and thought to himself, "It's not that time passes that matters. It's what time makes us leave behind."

Excited for Ten, William polished Smokey's saddle and brushed the horse down. William hitched Smokey to a new carriage Wils recently made. Wils noticed Ten coming out from the house with the winter bouquet in hand. He stood in the doorway of the blacksmith shop for just a moment and, also, thought of Lottie. He, too, remembered Lottie's love for the garden and wondered how she would be feeling about Ten's choice of girls.

Feeling uncomfortable, Ten was in his Sunday best as he stepped into the carriage feeling cleaner and shinier than he ever remembered. "You look mighty fine," Phietta smiled as she looked over her little brother as he sat straight and tall on the carriage seat. "Are you ready?" she asked. He nodded without a smile.

Wils smiled and said, "It will go well! I know it."

"I'm as ready as I will ever be!" Ten flicked the reins and Smokey headed out.

He took his time as he rode to the Rogers' place. He slowed down even more as he approached the house. He hopped off the carriage and swung the reins over the porch railing. Moving up the steps, Ten took a deep breath and knocked on the door. Harriet answered the door immediately as if she had been watching him ride up. Smiling too broadly, she greeted him with a sing-song voice, "Hello, Ten! Come on in." Ten stepped inside, forgetting the flowers in hand, and bumped them on the door jam. "Oops," he mumbled as he remembered them and held them up to his chest.

"Sarah, come now," Harriet called her daughter down from the loft. Sarah, also feeling very awkward, stumbled into the room as if someone from behind pushed her forward.

She turned her head away, frowned at someone behind her, and turned back, "Hi" Ten greeted her.

"Hello," Sarah responded. He smiled as she came into the room holding the winter bouquet behind him. They stepped outside to sit on the front porch for their first visit. It was chilly, and both were wearing heavy coats. She sulked and looked at her feet as they sat down. Awkwardly he handed her the flowers. She smiled, pleased to receive them, thinking, "Wow, Billy would never do this. I usually end up with grass in my hair."

"I sure think you are pretty, Sarah." Ten closed his eyes, wishing he hadn't said that. It was just that he didn't know what to say.

Embarrassed, she took a deep breath and said, "Humph."

"I know this is hard, but maybe we can visit a few times and you can get to know me better. I work hard, I'm smart and I'm a good farmer."

She humphed again.

Frustrated, Ten was not sure what to do next. He stood up and said, "Guess I'll be going now." He tipped his hat and slowly walked away, hoping she would call him back.

Sarah watched him leave and felt bad about being so rude, but not bad enough. "Maybe I'm not a good daughter." Sarah thought and was afraid to go back inside. This visit had not gone well.

Mother stepped out after Ten rode away. "How could you be so mean?"

"Ma, I don't even know him, let alone like him."

"Wasn't he nice and polite? The boys you like pull your hair and tease you. When they are Ten's age and ready to marry, they won't be interested in you at all. They will want pretty young girls just ready to become a woman like you are now!"

Sarah thought long and hard on that one. She already had seen friends dutifully marry older men that their parents chose. The men don't want older girls. Thinking to herself, "It just doesn't seem right. I should choose."

"You will see him again, and you will find that this man is kind, gentle, and very polite. Pa and I checked out his crops, and he does good work. The rows are straight, and the timber is cleared. We talked with Wils, his brother-in-law, you know the blacksmith down the road? Anyway, Wils thinks he is terrific. Wils said Ten stood by his pa and little brother when his ma died. He's a good man Sarah.

"I'll give him a second chance, Ma, but if I am to be a woman now, you must call me Sarah Jane."

Harriet smiled and thought that was an intriguing turn of attitude. "Okay, Sarah Jane."

The next visit was arranged by Sarah Jane's Ma and Pa. Ten was ready to drop the whole thing, so when they approached Ten the following Sunday and suggested a picnic, he was a bit surprised. Ten had wanted this to work, so he agreed to another visit. They planned a noon picnic down by the fire pit near the churchyard pond. It might be chilly, but it had been a warm winter so far. Phietta prepared the basket. Ten came by to pick Sarah Jane up with Smokey pulling the new-fangled carriage built by Wils. Sarah Jane was impressed by the carriage and loved the ride. She began to talk and babbled about silly things giggling as they rode. Ten took her for a ride by his fields. They were covered with snow now, but the timber was well-trimmed. She was impressed how well kept it all was, as her ma said she would be. They talked about their favorite trees, their favorite birds. They both agreed the Mockingbird was their favorite. They loved waking up to its endless string of bird songs, the first birds to sing in the morning and the last at night. "If not all night long." Ten joked. She told him she loved to sew and explained that she made her dresses and helped to make quilts at church. She told Ten she preferred to work in the garden the most. Ten listened. He loved listening to her voice. She had a pretty tone, full of optimism and energy, and he could sense her love to be with people. He was more of an introvert and envied that in her. Also, Ten didn't have to think about what to say; she filled all the quiet moments with chatter. They even talked about digging in the dirt, snatching and killing bugs, and pulling weeds. Sarah Jane went into vivid description describing how the aphids would leave a smear of green goo over the green leaves as she smashed them. They laughed and shared stories about "crazy bugs committing suicide by landing on their sweaty hands just waiting to be squashed." Ten used his right hand, pretending to dive bomb a fly sitting on his left hand, swatting it with a loud clap. Sarah Jane was surprised they could both laugh at such silly things. Ten was surprised he could be silly. He had been serious for so long.

Sarah Jane brought up how unhappy she had been about her Pa's decision to let him court her. "I told Ma; I am the one to decide who I will marry. Not him." Sarah Jane went on, "That's why I wasn't so nice when you came to visit the first time. I just don't like being told what to do. It had nothing to do with you."

Ten's eyes open wide, thinking, "My, she is feisty." But he tried to think the best of this, "I like that; she has spunk. A farmer needs that kind of woman by his side."

"Whew, Sarah, I thought it was me." Sarah Jane smiled in response, and he melted as she looked into his eyes. Sarah Jane kept looking deep into his eyes for the first time. She noticed how deep gray they were, and she marveled at the gold ring surrounding his pupils. The rings reminded her of the final glow of the sun against the darkness of nightfall. Her stomach fluttered, and she began to think this one might be all right.

Sarah Jane sat firmly and pressed her hands across her dress and spoke with conviction, "Well, I told Ma she had to call me Sarah Jane, now that I am a woman. So, I'd like you to call me Sarah Jane too."

Ten was silent as he looked at her. "That's it!" thought Ten, "that's the name Michael gave me!" He looked at this spirited young lady. Sarah Jane became uncomfortable with his long gaze; his eyes blinked, "Absolutely, Sarah Jane, it is!" Sarah Jane smiled and straightened her dress some more.

Each week they met. The two enjoyed Sunday afternoon carriage rides hoping for the sun to keep them warm. During their third meeting, she asked him a question. "Ten, I can't figure it out; why do they call you Ten?"

He laughed and responded, "It is a funny name, isn't it? I don't talk about it much." Then Ten thought to himself, "I don't talk much about it at all, except with you, it seems." He went on out loud, "My family knows why, and I guess no one else asked. When I was born, my mother was very proud that I was their tenth child. Pa wanted to name me after his grandfather. Ma wanted to call me Ten, so it became my middle name. My first name is weird and hard to spell, so I just stayed with Ten all this time.

Sarah Jane listened as he explained, "Well, I like it, 'cause it's different."

Sarah Jane was full of questions. He seemed to be interested in her ideas, and she was being treated like a woman now. She liked it and began thinking about issues and forming opinions on what folks at church were discussing, "What do you think of the women's temperance movement? I don't know much about it." and before he could respond, she went on, "I don't think it's all that big a deal. I don't see anyone drinking too much."

Ten spoke quietly, "Church folk don't drink. But I've seen a lot of drinking. As we left the army, many of my friends went crazy up in Chicago after they mustered out. They went to the saloon every night. I just wasn't interested. We never had any at the house, and I've not had time since the war. Don't know why one would have any at home." Then he went on, "Wils joined the Prohibition Party, and he strongly feels alcohol should not even be legal."

"Well, I think it's a waste of time and energy to get all stirred up about alcohol. Women have more important things to do. But I do think women are smart and should be able to vote." She hesitated and decided to say it anyway, "and choose their own husbands! We are human too!"

Ten laughed and smiled: "You sure are hard-headed. But you are a *pretty* hard-headed young lady!"

"Enough of that," flattered, Sarah Jane smiled and quickly changed the subject. When Ten mentioned the war, Sarah Jane wanted to know more about his experience. "Tell me about the war."

Ten said, "As Lincoln said, 'War at the best, is terrible, and this war of ours, in its magnitude and in its duration, is one of the most terrible'" Ten went on, "I liked that so much, I memorized it."

She prodded for more, "Did you have any fighting? Did you see confederates?" But she could not get him to talk any more about it.

An ugly memory stirred inside of him. "Stop." Ten thought intensely. After a moment, Ten finally said aloud, "One day I will tell you more. I need to wait a little longer until I know things are forever silent."

Although this made her more curious, Sarah Jane knew the subject was over for Ten and was quick to change the subject, "Ten, next time, how about you come over, and I will fix you a dinner."

Ten was surprised, "I like that idea!"

The Rogers family planned to go to church the evening Sarah Jane served Ten. However, after some discussion, it was decided her little brother Frank would stay back as the chaperone. Harriet wanted 17-year-old Joseph to stay back. But neither Joseph nor Sarah Jane was interested in that idea. Little Frank was a handful, and Harriet decided he would be an excellent choice to keep the young couple occupied.

Sarah Jane spent the afternoon preparing a chicken pie. Chicken pie was an exceptional treat for families in the 1860s, and that's what she decided to prepare. Sarah Jane set Frank up for a 'picnic' on the floor on the other side of the room, while she and Ten had the dinner table. She proudly carried the dish to the table as Ten sat there. Again, Ten was uncomfortable. He always came in from working the fields at the last minute after everyone else was seated. Lottie and Phietta would send someone out for him as the family often had already begun to sit down. He felt like a king as he sat and watched this beautiful young lady bring the chicken pie to him. She set the pie on the table and sat down slowly. She sat watching Ten intently as he slowly raised the fork to his mouth for the first bite. He chewed, and spontaneously, his eyes opened wide with delight. "This is wonderful! I've never had it before, but this is great!" Sarah Jane was pleased and burst into a huge grin. She was surprised and thankful that he was so supportive of her and the things she did. He made her feel like a princess, and she began to feel such warmth for this man. It was just a moment, but that moment had an impacted the rest of their lives.

"Ten, I know I was mean to you in the beginning. I am sorry. You are so kind to me. No one likes me the way you do."

Ten smiled, "I am glad to hear that, Sarah Jane. Maybe we can talk about what we want for our future." Sarah Jane looked puzzled. Ten looked over at Frank as the little boy ate his pie. "You seem to love kids. Do you want kids?"

"Why, of course, Ten. I want kids! I want a house with flowers in the front yard. I want to live on a farm with chickens and eggs, and cattle! I love to cook and put-up food for the winter. I sew and have no interest in the city."

Ten smiled and decided right then he would ask her parents for her hand in marriage very soon.

About that time, Frank finished his meal and, with a face covered with left over chicken pie, ran over to their table wanting to play. Sarah Jane laughed at the sudden change of conversation and got up convince Frank to help clear the table.

It was January, and Ten took the next day off and came by the Rogers house while the children were in school. He didn't want Sarah Jane around when he came by for this significant conversation with her folks. He was much less nervous this time, but he intended to follow proper procedure. He saw Jacob outside as he rode up on Smokey. Jacob waved, "Hello Ten, what you up to?"

Ten smiled and responded as he hopped off Smokey, "Wondered if I can have a word with you and Mrs. Rogers. Won't take long."

Jacob wiped his hands on his jeans and responded, "Sure Ten, Harriet's inside." Jacob walked on ahead and poked his head in the door. "Harriet, Ten is here and would like to speak with us." Both Jacob and Harriet knew what was coming. They had no interest in making this difficult for Ten. Harriet stepped outside; her apron covered with soot from cleaning out the cookstove. Jacob turned back to Ten as Harriet stood beside her husband.

"Well, folks. I think your daughter Sarah Jane is one fine young woman. You've done a great job raising her." Not wanting to delay any longer, Ten blurted out, "I'd surely would like your permission for her hand in marriage."

Harriet clapped her hands to her mouth and jumped, "Oh, Ten we would love that!" Then she stopped, regained her composure, and looked to Jacob for a proper response.

Jacob hesitated to recover the moment and smiled at Ten, "Ten, absolutely, we would love to have you marry Sarah Jane."

"Thank you, sir. I would greatly appreciate it if you don't tell her and let me ask her."

The parents smiled as Jacob responded, "Of course, we all know Sarah Jane must feel she has a decision in this matter, and that is the best way to handle it. You are a wise man." Harriet nodded to emphasize Jacob's point.

"I'll be asking her soon. Thank you again." Ten said as he nodded and headed back to Smokey.

A dance was scheduled at the church hall that coming weekend and Ten planned on asking Sarah Jane at the dance.

Arriving back at the Fierce place, Ten rode right up to the smith shop, hopped off Smokey, and strode up to the door. It was noisy as Wils was working the hot irons. Ten waited for Wils to pause, and at the first chance he could, Ten said loudly, "Wils." Wils looked up and saw Ten standing there. Ten seemed different, and Wils was instantly curious. Ten took a step forward, "Well, I did it." Wils looked puzzled and tilted his head waiting for more. "I asked the Rogers for Sarah Jane's hand in marriage."

Wils eyes opened wide, and he set his tools down grinning broadly as he walked up to Ten to pat him on the back. "Congratulations, Ten!" Wils was excited, grabbed Ten by the shoulders, turned him around, and said, "We must go tell Phietta. Now!"

Phietta jumped and squealed, "Ten, I am so happy for you!" By now, Ten was embarrassed and wanted desperately to go back to work. But Phietta went on with more questions, "When are you going to ask her? Do you have a ring?"

Ten tried to answer as fast as she asked, "This weekend at the dance."

"Yes, I bought it a while back. I just wasn't ready to take the leap 'til now."

Phietta went on, "Ten, you need a good bath, a haircut, and a good shave. I have some soap that will help with that. Give me your good clothes, and I'll make sure they are nice clean and for Friday night."

Sarah Jane had no idea what was coming. She noticed that her mother was a bit more interested in getting everyone pretty for the church dance. "Mother, why are we spending so much time fixing up the girls?"

"Well, Sarah Jane, January is always such a dull month; it's nice to have an excuse to look good. You need to fix yourself up too. What are you going to wear?" Enjoying the attention, Sarah Jane and Harriet spent Friday afternoon cleaning up all the family girls. Mary and Deborah were toddlers, but it was still fun dressing them up.

That night the dance seemed to be an enormous relief for most of the townsfolk. After the holidays, things always seemed drab and boring, and the locals always looked forward to their Winter Dance. Sarah Jane went with her family expecting to see Ten at the dance. She was surprised he was coming; he always seemed so shy about big group gatherings. But, he said he wanted to come to this dance. "Well, I will find out if he can dance," she thought to herself.

Ten arrived about half an hour after the Rogers. He and Smokey rode up behind Wils and Phietta's wagonful of kids. They were running a bit late as it took Wils and Phietta extra time to be sure Ten was as dressed up as nicely as he could be. Ten felt he was ready. Dreams of a future with his bride, Sarah Jane had drowned out the frightening visions of his visitor. Ten had not had a nightmare since their first date. The memories were still there, but only distant memories, and he was no longer dwelling on them. It had taken him eight and a half years to heal. It was a significant accomplishment. He did not want Sarah Jane to wake up to his cries in the night. It took Sarah Jane to help him heal, and she didn't even know it! Now, at 26 years, he had found his bride Sarah Jane, who had just turned 16. He was in love with this strong-minded and feisty young lady. He knew she could fully handle him, their children, and a life of farming in the west.

As they rode up to the church, he left his thoughts and watched the other folks still arriving, hoping to see Sarah Jane. He was so nervous, even though he was pretty sure she would say yes. This kind of thing was so foreign for him. "Why can't they make this process easier on us men?" he asked himself.

He helped Phietta down off the wagon as Wils unloaded the children. As a group, they all turned towards the fellowship hall that had been cleared and decorated for the dance. Chuck was already fiddling away inside, and the cheerful music drifted out into the churchyard. They joined the others as they walked through the darkness towards the lit-up fellowship hall.

Inside, Ten immediately saw Sarah Jane with her siblings gathered around her. They were looking over the refreshment table as Sarah Jane reviewing rules with the children regarding what and how much they could have. She looked up at the door hoping to see Ten, and there he was, smiling and watching her. Sarah Jane smiled back. She looked around, hoping to find a way to break away from her regular duties with the little ones. That's when Harriet stepped up. "Sarah Jane," Harriet took Frank's hand and smiled knowingly, "You go on and have a good time with Ten tonight. This is a dance, after all. I'll watch the little ones."

Sarah Jane smiled, "Thank you, Ma." and turned back and walked over to greet Ten.

"She looks so beautiful," thought Ten as she walked toward him. He patted his pocket to be sure the ring was still there. All was good.

"My he fixes up right nice," thought Sarah Jane as Ten waited for her.

"Hi, Ten, you got here."

"Yes, I had to help Wils and Phietta." He looked around, wondering what they would do now. It had been a very long time since he had been to a dance like this.

"Let's go look at the food table. Chuck just took a break and he's going to start up any minute. We should see what there is to eat before it's all gone." They didn't get to the table before Chuck began playing on his fiddle. Couples began filling the center of the room, ready to dance.

"Uh-oh." Ten thought, "Not sure I can do this." He struggled to follow the dance calls. They were new to him, but he did have good rhythm and was quick on his feet. After a couple of dances, he had it figured out and did well to keep up with Sarah Jane.

They danced until Chuck took a break and followed the crowd for some treats, hoping it wasn't all gone. Finding some cookies, they stepped outside to watch the bonfire that had been lit for the event. The fire's warmth on their faces countered the chill on their backs. They stood in silence, watching the flames as people gradually wandered back inside. Neither Ten nor Sarah Jane wanted to leave the glow of the fire.

Patiently, Ten waited for folks to disappear. Entranced, Sarah Jane watched the dancing flames and their crackling music. Once the music resumed and people headed back inside. After a few moments, Ten turned to Sarah Jane. "Sarah Jane," he looked at her. Dreamy from the fire's hypnotic trance, she looked at him. He had an odd look in his eyes. She thought to herself, "I think he had that look the first time he came to see me. I was so mean that day," she smiled and assured him, "Well, I won't be mean anymore."

He was lost, suddenly not knowing what to say. He had rehearsed his words so carefully as he rode Smokey to the church that evening. Smokey had even nodded as if to say, "Yes, I will!" He thought he was ready for this moment. "Sarah Jane," he said her name again and took her hands. "Thank God," he said to himself, he was sticking to plan.

She looked at him and began to realize what was going on. Her heart started to pound in her chest. "Oh, is this really going to happen?"

He looked at her and took in a deep breath, "Sarah Jane, I am a lucky man to have found you in my life. It is time to move on and build a future," He hesitated a moment to catch his breath, "and I would like to do that with you!" He paused again, and again he took a deep breath. Sarah Jane waited patiently. "Will you marry me?" Ten was astonished he remembered every word!

Sarah Jane clasped her hands to her face, "Yes!" she laughed and gave him their first kiss. Suddenly, cheering and clapping came from the church. Folks had gathered just outside the doorway to the dance hall, with Harriet and Jacob standing in the center. Wils and Phietta were right beside them. They had shared Ten's secret when the crowd resumed the dance and asked Chuck to keep playing while they went out to watch Ten and Sarah Jane in this very special moment. The young couple smiled back at the crowd. Ten suddenly remembered the ring. He pulled it out of his pocket and gestured for her to give him her hand. He slipped it on her finger. "Oh, and a ring too!" she gasped. The crowd roared another cheer.

The young couple looked up again to smile at their family and friends. That's when Ten saw him. He was standing behind the crowd, a head taller than anyone there. Michael smiled and nodded slightly. Ten smiled back, lifting his arm to wave as he stepped forward, but hesitated to look at Sarah Jane and take her hand. When he looked up again, Michael was gone.

Epilogue

Ten and Sarah Jane married on June 5, 1873. They farmed a short while in Illinois and welcomed a son in 1877 and a daughter in 1879. By 1880, they had their third son. Sarah Jane's parents and brother homesteaded in Kansas while the newlywed couple homesteaded in Nebraska shortly after the birth of their third son.

Wilson kept in touch by visiting and writing to Ten and Sarah Jane. (See Wils' letter to Ten written in 1886 in Historical Notes and Resources Section).

Sarah Jane wrote a diary during their years in Nebraska, writing about her children, grandchildren, and daily farm life in Southeast Nebraska. Her entries vividly describe the hard labor a farm family endured in those days. She mentions World War I, the arrival of their first automobile, a ringer washer, illnesses of family and friends, and World War II.

Ten and Sarah Jane's three children married and had families. Their youngest son stayed and helped on the farm. He was my grandfather.

On October 16, 1917, Ten attended the reunion of Union Soldiers at the "National Memorial Celebration and Peace Jubilee" in Vicksburg, Mississippi. Sarah Jane wrote in her diary:

October 13, 1917: Done Sat. work then dressed 2 chickens for Pa's meals while on train and baked beans.

October 14, 1917, Pa started to Vicksburg to the soldier's reunion. There were 18 soldiers from here.

Oct. 21, 1917, Pa got home at 2 AM.

Oct 22, 1917, Pa has a bad cold. Ten got back from Vicksburg Mississippi the 21ˢᵗ. He had a fine time.

The reunion menu is shown on the next page, showing that prunes were served every morning as a part of breakfast:

A Soldier's Dream, 1864

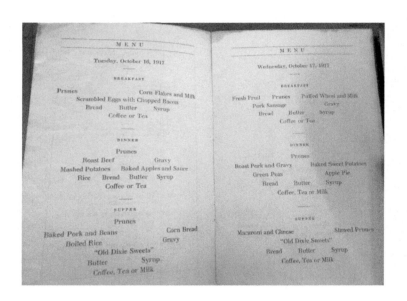

About the Author

Holly Bohling has a master's degree in Communication and is retired from an entrepreneurial career in program and business development serving people with disabilities, aging, and mental health. She has published and received awards for technical and research papers, however, her latent passion has always been her love for history and family lore. Bohling spent many hours listening to the stories of her grandparents, parents, aunts, uncles, and cousins.

Bohling imagines stories about life as she observes events evolving around her. Bohling is particularly fascinated by the relatively untold stories of her ancestors. By gathering family lore, photos, and historical family documents that have been saved for years, Bohling weaves a narrative of what life might have been like for her ancestors. She continues to study family history and the events of their time and imagines how their lives were impacted by their decisions in response to those events.

Acknowledgements

I would like to thank my family for their support as I pursued this project. My husband for his patience, the time he gave to review my work, and his honest feedback. My parents, siblings, cousins, grandparents, aunts, and uncles over time have been instrumental in helping me explore the life experience of our ancestors. They have been generous in sharing their stories, memories, and copies of family documents.

Holly Bohling

Historical Notes and Resource Materials

Primary sources include family historical documents, shared oral histories, photo albums, letters, saved documents.

Wareham Ten Gibbs' enrollment papers

Wareham Ten Gibbs' honorable discharge papers

A Soldier's Dream, 1864

Wareham Ten Gibbs' certificate of honorable service
signed by Abraham Lincoln

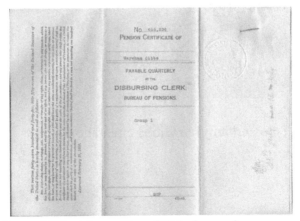

One of Wareham Ten Gibbs' pension papers

Wareham Ten Gibbs circa about 1928

1886 Letter from Wilson Fierce to Ten and Sarah Jane

1886

Cambridge J[u] Oct 24, 86

Mr & Mrs Gibbs

Through a well directed hand of Providence, I am able to write you a few ill Composed words. we are in reason health at home hoping this still messenger will find you & yours Enjoying the fruits of the Land Earned by honest Hands & no dark deeds to harness your peace in the future.

and Jno Jessie is not alive but just out of Eternity ready to sweep through the gates of Paradise she is now Waiting to meet the Savior in the Skies. I suppose

you have heared all about
the hail & wind Storm that
swept through hear on the
15 day of Aug, that upset
a great may / mens arrangemen
well it Just utterly tore
Rob all to flinders it tore
their Kitchen away & all
that was in it destroyed all
his Corn Crop it left hem
in destitue Circustances
Peter & I moved Jessie up
to my old house Sarah is
watting on her F E. Pierce paid
us a visit that is Katty & 2
Children But has returned
home stayed 18 day he is doing
well he wrote to Pratt if
he would deliver ther his
Col. Knox horse in good
shap they would give hem
$ 3 5 0. So Pratt will start

This Thursdy with the
horse Peter has two of
Sarahs Children. Clark
& Luella they are well pleasd
with the girl also she
sold Pete her land in
Fillmore County Neb,
for $ 1000 and sence she
sold it to Peter she Recd,
a deed from her Agent in
Neb. for her to sign for
$ 1200. E.E. Dill & family
arrived hear one week ago
Peter left for home on
monday & they got hear friday
aptr, they are well Expect
to stop all winter
Rodgers folks are all well
had a fine son Born Aug. 4
all doing well C.B. Morris
has built the finest house
south of Edwards

Ten how is the Corn Crop
& what is the price of Corn
Oats was good also grass
Corn is worth 30 ~~per bu~~
Oats 24 Hogs $3.50 Cattle
$2.50 to 9 good ones as
high as ever from $125.00 to
$2.00 - Butter 10 to 16 ct
per lb Eggs 15 Potatoes $1.00
Apples fall 25 to 50 ct per bu
turnips 75¢ Cabbage 10 bushel
no sale for shoats & young cattle
Write & let me know
all bout things in general
tell Elva & Hattie I often
think of them tell them to
go to school & write to Day
good By to all
Respectfully Wilson Fierce

Endnotes

[i] **Lance Herdegen, "Did the Midwest win the Civil War?"**
https://www.whatitmeanstobeamerican.org/places/did-the-midwest-win-the-civil-war/

[ii]   https://learnodo-newtonic.com/american-civil-war-effects

Ten Major Effects of the Civil War
The American Civil War remains the *deadliest battle for the country* with estimated deaths between *600,000 and 800,000.* The war claimed close to *50 percent more American lives than World War 2,* and *5 to 6 times more lives than World War 1.* The *Battle of Gettysburg* was the *bloodiest of all* claiming *close to 50,000 casualties* followed   by *Chickamauga* and *Spotsylvania. Diseases, infections and injury were the giant killers.* Wounded soldiers were housed in overfilled hospitals with filthy cownditions. The worst injuries were caused by

the *Minni   Ball* rifle   bullets   of *British Enfield* and *American   Springfield* rifles,   which were used extensively in the war. Conditions were *deplorable in   Union   and   Confederate prisons*, where *prisoners often died from outright neglect   or   starvation.* At the infamous *Camp Sumter* prison camp in *Georgia*, prisoners were described   as *"walking   skeletons".* The Camp Sumter prison claimed the life of *close to a fourth of its 45,000 prisoners.*

iii https://www.civilwarmed.org/ptsd/

Post-Traumatic Stress Disorder and the American Civil War

Post-battle carnage of Civil War. *Library of Congress*

iv

https://www.encyclopedia.com/history/enc yclopedias-almanacs-transcripts-and-maps/farmers-protest-movements-1870-1900-issue

After the American Civil War (1861–1865) agricultural prices began a long decline that lasted for a generation. Between 1870 and 1897 wheat fell from $106 per bushel to $63; corn fell from $43 to $29; and cotton fell from 15 cents a pound to five cents. At the same time farmers' costs of operation remained constant or increased. These costs included freight rates, interest on loans, and the cost of machinery and other needed commodities.

The cause of the farmers' troubles was overproduction occasioned by the expansion of the agricultural domain—it doubled during the same period—coupled with more efficient methods.

v

https://military.wikia.org/wiki/Illinois_in_t he_American_Civil_War

Illinois in the American Civil War
During the Civil War, 256,297 Illinoisians served in the Union army, more than any other northern state

except New York, Pennsylvania and Ohio. Beginning with Illinois resident President Lincoln's first call for troops and continuing throughout the war, the state mustered 150 infantry regiments, which were numbered from the 7th Illinois to the 156th Illinois. Seventeen cavalry regiments were also mustered, as well as two light artillery regiments.[1] Due to enthusiastic recruiting rallies and high response to voluntary calls to arms, the military draft was little used in Chicago and environs, but was a factor in supplying manpower to Illinois regiments late in the war in other regions of the state.

Camp Douglas, located near Chicago, was one of the largest training camps for these troops, as well as Camp Butler near Springfield. Both served as leading prisoner-of-war camps for captive Confederates. Another significant POW camp was located at Rock Island. Several thousand Confederates died while in custody in Illinois prison camps and are buried in a series of nearby cemeteries.

There were no Civil War battles fought in Illinois, but Cairo, at the juncture of the Ohio River with the Mississippi River, became an important Union supply base, protected by Camp Defiance. Other major supply depots were located at Mound City and across the Ohio river at Fort Anderson in Paducah, Kentucky, along with sprawling facilities for the United States Navy gunboats and associated river fleets. One of which would take part in the nearby Battle of Lucas Bend.

vi

Wareham Gibbs to Governor Trumbull during the Revolutionary War, 1775

Lieutenant Gibbs to Governour Trumbull.

Ticonderoga, October 10, 1775

Honored Sir: I being appointed to take down a number of sick people from this place to Connecticut, belonging to said Colony, and draw but two days' provisions from this place to Fort George, and when I came to Fort George, I could not get any provisions, salt nor fresh; and as I had no money, it put me and the sick soldiers into a very distressing situation but had the good fortune to borrow a little money. I got to Albany; and had it not been for Captain Phelps, we must all have suffered; but he let us have some money, though he said it was without orders; and I understand the General will not allow him a farthing of it; and he says he cannot pay any more to any body, as he has no money nor orders. And as I know our colony is humane, and would not have their friends die for want of provision and care, therefor think I couldn't not discharge my duty if I did not let your Honour know the situation of our sick - many obliged to sell their blankets and shirts to get bread, and others begging on the road. I beg there may be some provision made; if not, we must expect never to raise any more men. Our sick soldiers here are allowed four ounces of beef and one gill of rice per day.

Honoured Sir, forgive my freedom for letting you know the distress of the sick soldiers of our Colony. I shall be careful another year, and that is the universal say of all the officers.

I am, with respect, your Honour's very obedient humbler servant.

WAREHAM GIBBS, Lieutenant.

ⱽⁱⁱ Camp Fuller Hospital in Rockford, Illinois

This example of a former Civil War Hospital, renovated to serve as a hospital, sheltered wounded and suffering men in 1862. It was still standing in 2017. It should be noted, Simeon did not need care until 1864 and did not use this home.

Camp Fuller Hospital – 1928

📅 September 9, 2015   👤 Jan

Home That Helped Make History

These picturesque walls sheltered wounded and suffering men in 1862, when the house at 1260 N. Main st. saw service as a Civil war hospital for Camp Fuller. Rockford will be asked to help preserve this beautiful old home, at a tag day Saturday, under the auspices of Sons of Union Veterans and their auxiliary, who propose to purchase the building and convert it into a museum. Mrs. Emma Wolff, past department president of the S. U. V. auxiliary, will have charge of high school girls and others who will sell the tags. James C. Odell is chairman of the committee of John A. Logan post; S. U. V., which is sponsor for the tag day.

Source: Rockford Daily Republic newspaper May 3, 192ᶠ

Made in the USA
Las Vegas, NV
05 July 2021